THE PENG
FOUNDER EDITOR

KEVIN CROSSLEY-HOL... ... ...
writer for children. He was educated at Bryanston School
and St Edmund Hall, Oxford, and was Gregory Fellow in
Poetry at the University of Leeds (1969–71) and Lecturer
in Anglo-Saxon Literature and Culture for the Tufts-in-
London Program from its inception in 1967 to 1978. His
collections of poems include *The Rain-Giver* (1972) and
The Dream-House (1976), and he is translator of *The Battle
of Maldon and Other Old English Poems* (1965), *Beowulf*
(1968) and *Storm and Other Old English Riddles* (1970).
Among his books for children are *The Green Children*
(1966), winner of the Arts Council Award for the best
book for young children 1966–8, and *The Wildman* (1976),
winner of the Francis Williams Prize. His poems have appeared in numerous periodicals and newspapers, as have
his articles and reviews. Kevin Crossley-Holland has also
collaborated with a number of composers, including Sir
Arthur Bliss, who set to music some of the riddles in this
collection. He is now working on a retelling of the cycle
of *The Norse Myths*.

THE
EXETER BOOK
RIDDLES

Translated and Introduced by
Kevin Crossley-Holland

PENGUIN BOOKS

Penguin Books Ltd, Harmondsworth, Middlesex, England
Penguin Books, 625 Madison Avenue, New York, New York 10022, U.S.A.
Penguin Books Australia Ltd, Ringwood, Victoria, Australia
Penguin Books Canada Ltd, 2801 John Street, Markham, Ontario, Canada L3R 1B4
Penguin Books (N.Z.) Ltd, 182–190 Wairau Road, Auckland 10, New Zealand

—

This collection first published as *The Exeter Riddle Book* by
the Folio Society 1978
Published in Penguin Classics 1979
Copyright © Kevin Crossley-Holland, 1965, 1970, 1978
All rights reserved

Riddles 29, 30a, 47, 57, 77, 81 and 85
are reprinted by kind permission of
Novello & Co. Ltd

—

Made and printed in Great Britain
by Hazell Watson & Viney Ltd,
Aylesbury, Bucks
Set in Monotype Garamond

CONTENTS

INTRODUCTION

The nature of the riddle

The business of naming began with the Creation; the business of deceiving followed soon after, in the Garden of Eden. It is reasonable to suppose that as soon as men had wits they delighted in riddling. And they have delighted in it ever since: metaphor and simile, the detective story, the faked voice on the telephone, the crossword puzzle, the question in the cracker – they all hinge on recognition and, because they represent things as other than they are, they are all living members of the riddle family.

It was Aristotle who first put his finger on the similarity between riddle and metaphor. In his *Rhetoric*, he wrote:

While metaphor is a very frequent instrument of clever sayings, another or an additional instrument is deception, as people are more clearly conscious of having learned something from their sense of surprise at the way in which the sentence ends and their soul seems to say, 'Quite true and I had missed the point.' This, too, is the result of pleasure afforded by clever riddles; they are instructive and metaphorical in their expression.

Just so, and many of Aristotle's fellow countrymen are reputed to have lost their lives for being unable to answer the semi-metaphorical riddle: 'What has one voice, and goes on four legs in the morning, two legs in the afternoon, and three legs in the evening?' This is, of course, the famous enigma that the Sphinx, that fabulous winged beast with the head of a woman and the body of a lion, put to each passer-by as she sat by the precipice outside Thebes. Those who were unable to answer her she either devoured or hurled over the edge. And when Oedipus volunteered, 'It is man, who goes on all fours as a baby, who walks upright in the prime of his life, and who hobbles with a stick in old age,' the enraged Sphinx threw herself over the precipice.

We know that the ancient Egyptians, as well as the Greeks, liked riddling, and there are riddles in the first sacred book of the Brahmans, the *Rig Veda*. One of them depicts the year as a twelve-spoked wheel upon which stand 720 sons of one birth (the days and nights); and a comparable riddle turns up in an early Persian collection which describes knights (the days of the month) riding before the Emperor. These Time-Riddles are one of a number of universal riddle motifs – which is why they are also called 'World-Riddles' – and find their counterpart in the twenty-second riddle of the *Exeter Book*, 'The Month of December'. There are riddles in the *Koran*, too, and in the *Bible* there is, *inter alia*, the impossibly difficult riddle that Samson asked the Philistines at Timnah: 'Out of the eater came forth meat, and out of the strong came forth sweetness.' Delilah seduced Samson into telling her the answer (a honeycomb in the carcass of a dead lion) and paid Samson out by passing it on to the Philistines.

The word 'riddle' derives from the Old English *rædan*, to advise, to counsel, to guide, to explain. And in a wide sense a riddle does teach: it presents the old in new ways. To men sitting at the mead-bench, listening to the professional poet or taking the harp and improvising themselves, the riddle redefined the familiar. The Anglo-Saxon cast of mind and literary mode seems ideally suited to the metaphorical riddle when one considers that the entire body of Old English poetry is packed out with mini-riddles; they are known as 'kennings', and are in fact condensed metaphors. The sea is described as 'the swan's riding-place', 'the ship's road' and 'the whale's path'; a sail is spoken of as 'a sea-garment', a poet as 'a laughter-smith' and a wife as 'a peace-weaver'. Setting aside puns and conundrums and catch-questions, of which there are only a handful in the *Exeter Book*, what is a riddle but an extended kenning?

The Exeter Book

The first bishop of Exeter was Leofric. He died in 1072 and amongst his bequeathals to the Cathedral Library was *.i. mycel englisc boc be gehwilcum þingum on leoðwisan geworht*, 'one large book in English verse about various subjects'. This has always been taken to be the *Codex Exoniensis* or *Exeter Book*, one of the four great surviving miscellanies of Old English poetry. Probably copied by one scribe during the last quarter of the tenth century, this manuscript consists of 131 leaves or folios and contains a great range of poetry. There are 'documentary' Christian poems, such as 'Christ', which relates the Nativity and the Ascension and anticipates the Day of Judgement; there are Christian allegories about 'The Panther' and 'The Whale', which turn up again in many medieval bestiaries, and 'The Phoenix' (a godsend of a bird because of its supposed miraculous resurrection); there are elegiac poems, such as 'The Wanderer' and 'The Seafarer' (brilliantly translated by Ezra Pound), that are ostensibly Christian in their comparison of the transient life on earth with the eternal life in heaven, but which celebrate the old Germanic qualities of endurance and resilience, tempered by melancholy; there are poems such as 'Widsith' and 'Deor' that draw on the traditions and stories of the pagan Germanic world, survivals of the time before the Angles, Saxons, Frisians and Jutes first came to England; and, of course, there are the riddles. The *Exeter Book* is a remarkable anthology and, had it not survived, we would have to suppose the range of Old English poetry to be much narrower than we know it to be.

That the manuscript has survived seems virtually accidental. It is possible to deduce from gaps in the text that at least seven folios are missing. At some time it appears to have been used both as a cutting-board, perhaps a sort of bread-and-cheese board, and as a beer-mat; there are scores and circular stains on the first folio. More seriously, the manuscript has also been damaged by fire. A long diagonal burn on the last fourteen folios has destroyed the text of some of the later riddles, the last group of which are the final entry in the manuscript.

The number, condition, authorship, date of composition and sources of the riddles

There are ninety-six riddles in the *Exeter Book* and they have been copied into the manuscript in three groups: Riddles 1–59, Riddles 30b and 60, and Riddles 61–95. Because one folio is missing between Riddles 40 and 41 (see notes to those riddles) it is generally thought that, as with other earlier collections in Latin, there were originally one hundred riddles. It is the third group that has suffered because of the burn in the manuscript.

There is not, and is not likely to be, academic agreement over the authorship of the *Exeter Book* riddles. For a long time the eighth-century poet, Cynewulf, was believed to have composed them all. Now, conversely, most commentators suppose that the collection is the work of many hands, and that Cynewulf's was not one of them. In the words of Krapp and Dobbie, editors of *The Anglo-Saxon Poetic Records*, 'The question may, therefore, hardly be said to be definitely settled; but the burden of proof seems to be upon those who would demonstrate unity of authorship.' The date of composition is similarly uncertain, and all the more so because of the likelihood of multiple authorship, although there is linguistic evidence that a handful of the riddles were composed in the first half of the eighth century. In this context, Krapp and Dobbie write: 'It is of course very likely that a large number of the riddles date from the early eighth century, when Englishmen were most active in the composition of Latin riddles, but a more definite statement than this is hardly possible in the light of our present knowledge.'

Who were these English riddlers writing in Latin, and what bearing do they have on the *Exeter Book* collection? The first question is easy to answer, the second not so. There are three surviving collections in Latin. They are ascribed to Aldhelm (*c.* 640–709), who was Abbot of Malmesbury and subsequently Bishop of Sherborne, and who wrote one hundred riddles or *Ænigmata*; to Tatwine (d. 734), who was an Archbishop of Canterbury; and to Eusebius (*c.* 680–*c.* 747), who is believed to be one and the same as Hwætberht, Abbot of Wearmouth and a friend of Bede. The riddles by Tatwine and Eusebius are preserved in the same manuscript and together number one hundred – Tatwine was responsible for forty and Eusebius sixty. Aldhelm acknowledges as his model Symphosius, whose collection of one hundred riddles also survives, and who is credited with originating the literary riddle in post-Classical times. He is thought to have lived in the late fourth or early fifth century.

Much valuable work has been done recently on the sources and analogues of the riddles, and it is clear that the three collections by Englishmen and the earlier collection by Symphosius were all known to the *Exeter Book* riddlers. In one or two cases, for example Riddle 40 (see Notes), the Anglo-Saxon riddler attempted a translation and elaboration of the Latin original; in several instances the correspondence between Old English and Latin is so close that the Latin can be taken as a source; while in a number of other cases the Anglo-Saxon riddler either borrowed and very freely developed an idea in one of the Latin riddles, or else both Anglo-Saxon and Latin riddles are analogues, referring to the same traditional material. In so far as possible, the Notes to the riddles identify any known Latin source or analogue.

It should not be supposed, though, that the *Exeter Book* riddles are a collection of half-baked derivations. On the contrary they have great imaginative zest, great charm, and at times great subtlety; they are a wonderfully attractive collection of riddles in their own right.

The elements of the collection

In many ways the riddles constitute a delightful and informative entrée into the Anglo-Saxon world. Some are folkriddles (distinguished by their use of popular material, their shortness and simplicity), some are literary riddles (full of conscious poetic elaboration and attention to detail), and some combine both elements. Just as the tone and treatment varies from one riddle to the next, so does the subject-matter itself. As one turns from natural phenomena to animal and bird life, from the Christian concept of the Creation to humdrum domestic objects, from weaponry to the peaceful pursuits of writing and music, one wins glimpse after glimpse of the Anglo-Saxons and their attitudes.

It may be worth looking at the elements of the collection in a little more detail. Typically enough, more than a dozen riddles are concerned with weapons and war-gear and contest – sword, for instance, and shield, bow, battering ram. This is what one would expect of a society caught up in almost endless turmoil – against the Romano-British, against each other, against the Vikings and, finally, against the Normans. It was a society whose values had changed very little despite migration from the European Continent, the advent of Christianity and the passage of time. Describing the way of life of the German tribes living within the Roman Empire in the first century, Tacitus noted in his *Germania*: 'As for leaving a battle alive after your chief has fallen, that means lifelong infamy and shame. To defend and protect him, to put down one's own acts of heroism to his credit – that is what they really mean by allegiance. The chiefs fight for victory, the companions for their chief.' And again: 'A man is bound to take up the feuds as well as the friendships of father or kinsman.' The bond between chief and followers, the emphasis on kinship, on physical and moral courage and on the blood-feud were just as important to the Anglo-Saxons at the Battle of Hastings as to their Germanic ancestors in the first century. These are the tremendous words of Byrhtwold at the end of 'The Battle of Maldon' (fought in 991) after his lord has been slain and the Danes, the war-wolves, are on the brink of victory:

> Mind must be the firmer, heart the more fierce,
> courage the greater, as our strength diminishes.
> Here lies our leader, dead,
> an heroic man in the dust.
> He who now longs to escape will lament for ever.
> I am old. I will not go from here,
> but I mean to lie by the side of my lord,
> lie in the dust with the man I loved so dearly.

The deserter was condemned to live an unenviable life of exile, and the fundamental lord-retainer relationship is touched on in several of the riddles. So too is the overriding sense of *wyrd* – fate – and the need to struggle against it, which dogged the pagan tribes that first came to England and their descendants, the Anglo-Saxons. This was a society whose greatest ambition was for fame despite all; the last word of *Beowulf* describes that hero as *lofgeornost*, 'most eager for fame'. One of the Old Norse sayings attributed to Odin, very nicely sums up the pagan Anglo-Saxon's attitude to life: 'One thing I know never dies or changes, the reputation of a dead man.'

Just as some riddles in the *Exeter Book* reflect aspects of the Germanic heroic world, others describe objects, such as the *Bible* and chalice, associated with the new Christian faith that swept through England during the seventh century. One can visualize what hope Christian teaching must have brought, the hope of a life after death. Nothing exemplifies it quite as well as the much-quoted words of one of King Edwin's councillors (related by Bede), when that King was considering whether or not to adopt the new Christian faith:

O King, imagine you are sitting at a banquet with your ealdor-men and thanes in winter time; the fire is burning and the hall is warm, and outside the winter storms are raging; and there should come a sparrow flying swiftly through the hall, coming in through one door and out by another. While it is inside, it is safe from the winter storms; but after a few minutes of comfort, it soon returns from winter back to winter again, and is lost to sight. Likewise, this mortal life seems like a short interval; what may have come before, or what may come after it, we do not know. Therefore, O King, if this new Christian teaching brings any greater certainty, it seems fitting that we should follow it.

King Edwin followed it!

During the seventh and eighth centuries, the scriptoria of the great Northumbrian monasteries produced a steady stream of manuscripts (see Note to Riddle 26), for use at home and for missionary activity on the Continent. There are several riddles about the work of the scribe, the illumination of manuscripts, and the custody of books – including a charming short poem about a bookmoth – while another group of riddles is concerned with musical instruments that would have been heard inside and outside the monastery: harp, horn, reed-flute and bagpipe.

Although the *Exeter Book* riddles reflect aspects of Germanic heroism and of Christianity, in either case quite formal and dignified, the foremost preoccupation of the collection is with the everyday life of working people, with household objects, and with aspects of the natural world. There are riddles about bucket and bellows, churn and key, ale and mead, anchor and plough; riddles about badger and bullock, the swan, the jay, the swallow, the copulating cock and hen; riddles about the sun and moon, and sudden storms, and ice. They are informed by sharp observation, charm, an earthy sense of humour, above all by a sense of wonder – and they make us in turn recognize that every object around us has its distinctive attributes and a life of its own. Even if the riddlers were clerics (as they doubtless were) the majority of the riddles reflect the views of people who may have been aware of fate and of God, and struggled manfully to reconcile the two, but were in the end more concerned with crops than concepts. The Anglo-Saxons were above all an agricultural people and, more than any other literature that survives from the period, this riddle collection is the song of the unsung labourer.

In surveying the constituents of the *Exeter Book* collection, it only remains to mention the six runic riddles. Rune means 'mystery' or 'secret' and the runic alphabet is thought to have originated at the beginning of the Christian era. It consisted of twenty-four letters (known as the *futhark*) and each letter had its name and meaning: the letter D, for instance, is represented by ⋈ in the runic alphabet, and its name was *dæg*, 'day'. Gwyn Jones writes in *A History of the Vikings*: 'The shape of its letters, based on vertical and diagonal strokes, and avoiding horizontals and curves, suggests this was an alphabet designed for use on wood.' It was first used for magical purposes but was used more generally in Anglo-Saxon England, sometimes for protective purposes (runes engraved on a sword blade, for example), and sometimes for identification. The *Exeter Book* riddlers used runes instead of, or as well as, poetic ambiguity – a kind of additional conundrum.

It is with these runic riddles, and with the punning Riddle 30a, that the *Exeter Book* collection comes closest to the catch-question riddle that has doubtless prospered in every age, and that most children have up their sleeves today – the riddle more concerned with the value of words than with the object described. This kind of riddle must have reached its apogee with the Victorians: Why is a good meerschaum like a water-colour artist? *Because it draws and colours beautifully*. Why has the Dark Continent no terrors for Mr Stanley? *Because he 'makes light' of it*. What part of a fish is like the end of a book? *Don't you know? Why, the fin-is*. Teasers of this kind can be fun and they can be extremely boring. But either way they are devoid of poetry. The glory of the *Exeter Book* collection is that it consists of riddles which are, at their best, excellent enigmas *and* excellent poems.

Principles of translations and arrangements of the volume

All Old English poetry, and about 30,000 lines survive, was composed in stately, pounding four-stress lines, with at least two of the stresses (one of them invariably the third) emphasized by alliteration. The vocabulary of the poet was formal; it made use of many compounds and of the kennings to which I have already alluded. The language of the poet, no less highly wrought than the work of the jeweller, must have seemed to the Anglo-Saxons just as artificial as Spenser's language did to Elizabethan ears. The difference is that Anglo-Saxon poets were working within an oral tradition.

In translating these riddles, I have settled for a non-syllabic four-stress line, controlled by light alliteration. My diction inclines to the formal – although it is by no means as highly wrought as that of the original poets. I have understood my first duty as a translator (as opposed to an imitator) to be to convey the actual meaning of the Anglo-Saxon, and have with respect tried to follow the example set by Alfred, who wrote in his Preface to Gregory's *Pastoral Care* that he translated *hwilum worde be worde, hwilum andgit of andgiete*, 'Sometimes word for word, sometimes sense for sense'. But I have also pursued the elusive spirit of the originals, and if some of the translations are also thought to read as poems in their own right, so much the better.

In this volume, the main text includes translations of seventy-five of the ninety-six *Exeter Book* riddles – all those that are not either very badly damaged or impossibly obscure. The original numbering of the riddles has been adopted, and this means that the main text has a broken sequence of numbers. The Notes at the end of the book deal with all the riddles consecutively and include translations of sixteen of the remaining riddles. No translations are offered for the remaining five riddles for reasons stated in the notes on them.

Acknowledgements

I have translated from the text of the standard edition of *The Exeter Book (Anglo-Saxon Poetic Records III)*, edited by George Philip Krapp and Elliot van Kirk Dobbie (New York, 1936). In discussing possible solutions, it will be evident that I have made use of the meticulous summaries prepared by Krapp and Dobbie, and have also taken particular account of the opinions expressed in *The Riddles of the Exeter Book*, edited by Frederick Tupper (Boston, 1910), *Old English Riddles*, edited by A. J. Wyatt (Boston, 1912), and *Anglo-Saxon Riddles of the Exeter Book*, translated by Paull F. Baum (Durham, North Carolina, 1963). When I have provided a solution to a riddle without equivocation, it means that all commentators have agreed upon it. I must also acknowledge my extensive use of *Sources and Analogues of Old English Poetry*, translated by Michael J. B. Allen and Daniel G. Calder (Cambridge, 1976).

Some of the riddles in this volume were first published in my translations of *The Battle of Maldon and Other Old English Poems* (London, 1965) and *Storm and Other Old English Riddles* (London, 1970), and I have made some use both of the latter and of my history of the Anglo-Saxons, *Green Blades Rising* (London, 1974), in preparing this Introduction and the Notes.

I began to translate the Old English riddles shortly before coming down from Oxford in 1962. This book therefore celebrates a fifteen-year involvement, and I cannot fully acknowledge the stimulus and assistance so many people have given me over that period. There are, though, some friends whom I must thank now in public and particular. Bruce Mitchell, my tutor and then my collaborator, first excited and unobtrusively guided my adult interest in the Anglo-Saxons and their literature, and he offered me line-by-line criticism of the translations of many of these riddles; George MacBeth gave me a BBC platform for the first group of riddles I translated; and Sir Arthur Bliss provided a great stimulus by setting some of them to music. I have discussed the translations and possible solutions with many friends, and owe a special debt to Marni Hodgkin for helping to shape *Storm and Other Old English Riddles* and to Richard Barber for his most helpful critical suggestions over a number of years. Val Kwaan offered valuable criticism of the Introduction; Rosamond Richardson has given me generous support and encouragement when it mattered; and lastly I sincerely thank John Letts, whose idea it was that I should translate the *Exeter Book* riddles entire.

KEVIN CROSSLEY-HOLLAND

THE RIDDLES

I

Which man is so sharp and so quick-witted
as to guess who goads me on my journey
when I get up, angry, at times awesome;
when I roar loudly and rampage over the land,
sometimes causing havoc; when I burn houses
and ransack palaces? Smoke rises,
ashen over roofs. There is a din on earth
and men die violently when I shake the forest,
the flourishing trees, and fell timber –
I with my roof of water, driven far and wide
in pursuit of vengeance by the powers above;
I carry on my back what once covered
every man, body and soul submerged
together in the water. Say what conceals me
or what I, who bear this burden, am called.

2

Sometimes I plunge through the press of waves
unexpectedly, delving to the earth,
the ocean bed. The waters ferment,
sea-horses foaming . . .
The whale-mere roars, fiercely rages,
waves beat upon the shore; stones and sand,
seaweed and saltspray, are savagely flung
against the dunes when, wrestling
far beneath the waves, I disturb the earth,
the vast depths of the sea. Nor can I escape
my ocean bed before he permits me who is my pilot
on every journey. Tell me, wise man:
who separates me from the sea's embrace,
when the waters become quiet once more,
the waves calm which before had covered me?

3

Sometimes my Lord corners me;
then He imprisons all that I am
under fertile fields – He frustrates me,
condemns me in my might to darkness,
casts me into a cave where my warden, earth,
sits on my back. I cannot break out
of that dungeon, but I shake halls
and houses; the gabled homes of men
tremble and totter; walls quake,
then overhang. Air floats above earth,
and the face of the ocean seems still
until I burst out from my cramped cell
at my Lord's bidding, He who in anger
buried me before, so shackled me that I
could not escape my Guardian, my Guide.

Sometimes I swoop to whip up waves, rouse
the water, drive the flint-grey rollers
to the shore. Spuming crests crash
against the cliff, dark precipice looming
over deep water; a second tide,
a sombre flood, follows the first;
together they fret against the sheer face,
the rocky coast. Then the ship is filled
with the yells of sailors; the cliffs quietly
abide the ocean's froth and fury,
lashing waves, racing rollers
that smash against stone. The ship must face
a savage battle, a bitter struggle,

if the sea so buffets it and its cargo
of souls that it is no longer under control
but, fighting for life, rides foaming
on the spines of breakers. There men see
the terror I must obey when I bluster
on my way. Who shall restrain it?

At times I rush through the dark clouds
that ride me, churn the sea into a frenzy,
then afterwards let the water subside.
When one cloud collides with another,
edge against sharp edge, the din
of destruction, a mighty noise, echoes
above the dwellings of men; dark bodies,
hastening, breathe fire overhead,
flashing lightning; thunderous crashes
shake the sky, then growl darkly.
The clouds do combat, dark drops
fall, rustling rain from their wombs.
A fear-tide flows in the hearts of men,
a growing terror – strongholds succumb
to dread – when that ghastly troop goes
on the rampage, and shrithing evil spirits,
spurting flames, shoot sharp weapons.
A fool is unafraid of the death-spears,
but for all that he will die
if the true Lord lets fly the arrow,
a whistling weapon, straight through rain
from the whirlwind above. Few men
survive, if they are struck by lightning.
I am the origin of all that strife,
when I rush through the concourse of clouds,
surge forward with great strength, and fly
over the face of the water. Troops on high

clash noisily; then, afterwards,
under cover of night, I sink to earth,
and carry off some burden on my back,
renewed once more by my Lord's power.
I am a mighty servant: sometimes
I fight, sometimes wait under the earth;
at times I swoop and sink under water,
at times whip up waves from above;
sometimes I rise, stir up trouble
amongst scudding clouds; swift and savage,
I travel widely. Tell me my name,
and Who it is rouses me from my rest,
or Who restrains me when I remain silent.

4

Ring me, they ring me. I work long hours
and must eagerly obey my thane,
break my rest, and loudly proclaim
that my guardian gave me a halter.
A man or a woman, weary and bleary,
has often called on me; winter-cold
I answer them, surly as they are. Sometimes
a warm limb releases the bound ring.
But it delights my thane, a dull sort
of man, and satisfies me into the bargain,
if anyone can fathom and solve my riddle.

5

I'm by nature solitary, scarred by spear
and wounded by sword, weary of battle.
I frequently see the face of war, and fight
hateful enemies; yet I hold no hope
of help being brought to me in the battle,
before I'm eventually done to death.
In the stronghold of the city sharp-edged swords,
skilfully forged in the flame by smiths,
bite deeply into me. I can but await
a more fearsome encounter; it is not for me
to discover in the city any of those doctors
who heal grievous wounds with roots and herbs.
The scars from sword wounds gape wider and wider;
death blows are dealt me by day and by night.

6

Christ, who alone ordains victories,
created me for combat. When my lord
urges me to fight, I often scorch mortals;
I approach the earth and, without a touch,
afflict a huge host of people.
At times I gladden the minds of men,
keeping my distance I console those
whom I fought before; though in that consolation
they're aware of the conflict also when, once more,
after such suffering I soothe their lives.

7

Silent is my dress when I step across the earth,
reside in my house, or ruffle the waters.
Sometimes my adornments and this high windy air
lift me over the livings of men,
the power of the clouds carries me far
over all people. My white pinions
resound very loudly, ring with a melody,
sing out clearly, when I sleep not on
the soil or settle on grey waters – a travelling spirit.

8

I've one mouth but many voices;
I dissemble and often change my tune;
I declaim my deathless melodies,
I don't desist from my refrain.
Aged evening-songster, I entertain
men in their homes by rehearsing
my whole repertoire; they sit, bowed down,
quiet in their houses. Guess my name,
I who mimic the jester's japes
as loudly as I can, and rejoice men
with choicest songs in various voices.

9

In former days my mother and father
forsook me for dead, for the fullness of life
was not yet within me. But another woman
graciously fitted me out in soft garments,
as kind to me as to her own children,
tended and took me under her wing;
until under shelter, unlike her kin,
I matured as a mighty bird (as was my fate).
My guardian then fed me until I could fly,
and could wander more widely on my
excursions; she had the less of her own
sons and daughters by what she did thus.

10

My beak was bound and I was immersed,
the current swept round me as I lay covered
by mountain streams; I matured in the sea,
above the milling waves, my body
locked to a stray, floating spar.
When, in black garments, I left the waves
and the wood, I was full of life;
some of my clothing was white
when the tides of air lifted me,
the wind from the wave, then carried me far
over the seal's bath. Say what I am called.

II

My garb is ashen and in my garments
bright jewels, garnet-coloured, gleam.
I mislead muddlers, despatch the thoughtless
on fool's errands, and thwart cautious men
on their useful journeys. I can't think
why, addled, led astray, and robbed
of their senses, men should praise my crooked ways
wherever they go. Woe betide addicts
when they bring the dearest of hoards on high
unless they've quite foregone their foolish habits.

12

I travel by foot, trample the ground,
the green fields, for as long as I live.
Lifeless, I fetter dark Welshmen,
sometimes their betters too. At times
I give a warrior liquor from within me,
at times a stately bride steps on me;
sometimes a slave-girl, raven-haired,
brought far from Wales, cradles and presses me –
some stupid, sozzled maidservant, she fills me
with water on dark nights, warms me
by the gleaming fire; on my breast
she places a wanton hand and writhes about,
then sweeps me against her dark declivity.
What am I called who, alive, lay waste
the land and, dead, serve humankind?

I saw ten in all, roaming the greensward,
six brothers strutting with their sisters;
they had living spirits. A garment of skin –
there was no mistaking it – hung on the wall
of each one's house. And none were worse off,
nor their movements more painful, though
they must gnaw at the grey-green shoots,
robbed of their garments, roused by the might
of the guardian of heaven. New clothing
is furnished for those who before walked out
naked; they scatter and roam over the land.

14

I was once a warrior's weapon.
Now a noble young retainer
dresses me in threads of twisted gold
and silver. At times men kiss me,
at times I summon close friends
to do battle; a horse sometimes bears me
over the earth, sea-horses sometimes
sweep me, gleaming, over the ocean;
now and then a maiden, ring-adorned,
replenishes my paunch. I must lie on planks
at times, plundered, hard and headless;
often, gold-garbed, I hang on the wall
above drinking warriors, a splendid sight,
instrument of war. Covered in riches
I draw in breath from a brave man's lungs
when retainers ride towards battle.
At times I tell proud warriors
that wine is served; at times rally them,
save booty from hostile men, drive off
the enemy. Now ask me my name.

15

Whereas my neck is white, my head
and sides are brown; I'm swift of movement
and bear a battle-weapon; hair covers my back
and my cheeks as well; two ears tower high
above my eyes. I step on my toes through
the green grass. Grief is ordained for me
if any fierce creature should catch me
in my hole where I have my house and children,
and if we linger any longer there
when this uninvited guest, the harbinger
of death, comes knocking at my door.
I must courageously carry my infants
far from our house, and save them by flight,
if that creature continues to follow me.
He advances on his breast. I dare not await him
in my hole . . . that were not a wise plan at all.
I must burrow through the steep hillside
with my two forefeet as fast as I can.
I can save the lives of my loved ones
with ease, once I've guided them out
by a secret way through a hole in the hill.
Then, if it comes to blows and battle
I feel no fear of this murderous foe.
Should he persist in chasing me
through that narrow hole I've just made in the hill,
I will not fail to fight him fiercely.
Once I've tunnelled my way to the top,
I will angrily batter my enemy,
that hateful foe from whom I long fled.

16

I must fight with the waves whipped up by the wind,
contending alone with their force combined,
when I dive to earth under the sea.
My own country is unknown to me.
If I can stay still, I'm strong in the fray.
If not, their might is greater than mine:
they'll break me in fragments and put me to flight,
intending to plunder what I must protect.
I can foil them if my fins are not frail,
and the rocks hold firm against my force.
You know my nature, now guess my name.

17

Confined by a wire fence, filled
with brave treasures, I'm the bulwark
of my people. Many is the morning
I spew spear-terror; the more I'm fed,
the greater my strength. My guardian controls
the flight of arrows from my belly.
At times I almost swallow the burnished
dark bolts, the baleful weapons,
searing poisoned spears, esteemed by warriors.
A man remembers what issues from my mouth.

I'm a strange creature, shaped for a scrap,
dear to my lord, finely decorated.
My clothing is motley and bright metal threads
mount the deadly jewel my master
gave me – the man who at times involves me
in a fight. I carry treasure then,
the handiwork of smiths, gold in the court,
all the clear day. I often despatch
well-armed warriors. A king enriches me
with silver and precious stones, honours me
in the hall; he doesn't stint but sings my praises
to the gathering – men swigging mead;
at times he holds me in reserve, at times
sets me free, travel-weary, eager
in the fray. Often I set friend
at the throats of friends; I'm widely reviled,
the most accursed of weapons. If a cruel warrior
should assault me in battle, I cannot hope
for a son to avenge me on my slayer;
nor will the family from which I sprang
be increased through children of mine
unless, lordless, I have to leave
the guardian who once gave me rings.
If I follow a warrior and fight on his behalf,
as I've done before for my master's satisfaction,
I must forego, as fate wills, the chance
to father children. I cannot lie
with a woman, but the same man who once
bound me with a belt denies me now

the rapture of loveplay; I must enjoy
the treasure of heroes single and celibate.
Tricked out with metal threads, I often
irritate and frustrate some woman; she insults me,
smacks her hands and runs me down,
yells abuses. This is not my kind of contest . . .

I keep my snout to the ground; I burrow
deep into the earth, and churn it as I go,
guided by the grey foe of the forest
and by my lord, my stooping owner
who steps behind me; he drives me
over the field, supports and pushes me,
broadcasts in my wake. Brought from the wood,
borne on a wagon, then skilfully bound,
I travel onward; I have many scars.
There's green on one flank wherever I go,
on the other my tracks – black, unmistakable.
A sharp weapon, rammed through my spine,
hangs beneath me; another, on my head,
firm and pointing forward, falls on one side
so I can tear the earth with my teeth
if my lord, behind me, serves me rightly.

22

Sixty men in company came
riding down to the estuary. Eleven
of those mounted men had horses
of peace, and four had pale grey horses.
The warriors could not cross the water
as they wished for the channel was too deep,
the shelf too abrupt, the current too strong,
the choppy waves thronging. Then the men
and their horses climbed on to a waggon – a burden
under the cross-bar; and then a single horse
hauled those proud spear-warriors with their steeds,
dragged the waggon right across the estuary,
although no ox, nor carthorse, nor muscular men
dragged it with him; and he did not swim,
nor wade on the bottom because of his guests' weight,
nor muddy the water, nor ride on the wind,
nor double back. Rather, he carried
the warriors and their horses across the creek
from the steep bank, the staithe, so that they
stepped up bravely on the opposite side,
men and their mounts unscathed by water.

Wob's my name, if you work it out;
I'm a fair creature fashioned for battle.
When I bend, and shoot a deadly shaft
from my stomach, I desire only to send
that poison as far away as possible.
When my lord, who devised this torment for me,
releases my limbs, I become longer
and, bent upon slaughter, spit out
that deadly poison I swallowed before.
No man's parted easily from the object
I describe; if he's struck by what flies
from my stomach, he pays for its poison
with his strength – speedy atonement for his life.
I'll serve no master when unstrung, only when
I'm cunningly notched. Now guess my name.

24

I'm a strange creature with various voices:
I can bark like a dog, bleat like a goat,
honk like a goose, shriek like a hawk,
at times I imitate the ashen eagle,
the battle-bird's cry; the vulture's croak
trips off my tongue, and the mew of the seagull,
as I sit here, saucily. G suggests
my name, and Æ, R and O assist it,
so do H and I. I'm called
what these six characters clearly spell out.

I'm a strange creature, for I satisfy women,
a service to the neighbours! No one suffers
at my hands except for my slayer.
I grow very tall, erect in a bed,
I'm hairy underneath. From time to time
a beautiful girl, the brave daughter
of some churl dares to hold me,
grips my russet skin, robs me of my head
and puts me in the pantry. At once that girl
with plaited hair who has confined me
remembers our meeting. Her eye moistens.

An enemy ended my life, deprived me
of my physical strength; then he dipped me
in water and drew me out again,
and put me in the sun where I soon shed
all my hair. After that, the knife's sharp edge
bit into me and all my blemishes were scraped away;
fingers folded me and the bird's feather
often moved over my brown surface,
sprinkling meaningful marks; it swallowed more wood-dye
(part of the stream) and again travelled over me
leaving black tracks. Then a man bound me,
he stretched skin over me and adorned me
with gold; thus I am enriched by the wondrous work
of smiths, wound about with shining metal.
Now my clasp and my red dye
and these glorious adornments bring fame far and wide
to the Protector of Men, and not to the pains of hell.
If only the sons of men would make use of me
they would be the safer and the more victorious,
their hearts would be bolder, their minds more at ease,
their thoughts wiser; and they would have more friends,
companions and kinsmen (courageous, honourable,
trusty, kind) who would gladly increase
their honour and prosperity, and heap
benefits upon them, ever holding them
most dear. Ask what I am called,
of such use to men. My name is famous,
of service to men and sacred in itself.

27

Favoured by men, I am found far and wide,
taken from woods and the heights of the town,
from high and from low. During each day
corbiculas brought me through the bright sky
skilfully home to a safe shelter. Soon after that
I was taken by men and bathed in a tub.
Now I bind and I chasten them, and cast
a young man at once to the ground, and sometimes an old one
     too.
He who struggles against my strength,
he who dares grapple with me, discovers immediately
that he will hit the hard floor with his back
if he persists with such stupidity.
Deprived of his strength, and strangely loquacious,
he's a nincompoop, who rules neither his mind
nor his hands nor his feet. Now ask me, my friends,
who knocks young men stupid, and as his slaves binds them
in broad, waking daylight? Yes, ask me my name.

Some acres of this middle-earth
are handsomely attired with the hardest, sharpest,
most bitter of man's fine belongings;
it is cut, threshed, couched, kilned,
mashed, strained, sparged, yeasted,
covered, racked, and carried far
to the doors of men. A quickening delight
lies in this treasure, lingers and lasts
for men who, from experience, indulge
their inclinations and don't rail against them;
and then, after death, it begins to gab,
to gossip recklessly. Shrewd men
must think carefully what this creature is.

29

I saw a strange creature,
a bright ship of the air beautifully adorned,
bearing away plunder between her horns,
fetching it home from a foray.
She was minded to build a bower in her stronghold,
and construct it with cunning if she could do so.
But then a mighty creature appeared over the mountain
whose face is familiar to all dwellers on earth;
he seized on his treasure and sent home the wanderer
much against her will; she went westward
harbouring hostility, hastening forth.
Dust lifted to heaven; dew fell on the earth,
night fled hence; and no man knew
thereafter, where that strange creature went.

30a

I'm surrounded by flames and sport with the wind,
I'm clothed with finery and the storm's great friend,
ready to travel, but troubled by fire,
a glade in full bloom and a burning flame;
friends often pass me from hand to hand,
and I'm kissed by ladies and courteous men.
But when I raise myself, with reverence
proud men must bow to me; I bring
man's happiness to full maturity.

This world is adorned in diverse
ways, decorated with rare ornaments.
I saw a strange thing singing in a house;
nothing on earth looked in the least
like this creature, her shape was extraordinary.
Her beak was pointed downwards;
yet she cannot fly nor even move much,
though eager to start she sets to work
with her singular skills; often and again
she goes the rounds at gatherings of men,
she sits at the feast and awaits her turn –
it comes soon – to prove her prowess
in the halls of thanes. But there this creature
never partakes of what makes warriors happy.
Daring, anxious for fame, she stays dumb;
and yet in her foot she has a fine voice,
the glorious gift of song. I find it
curious that this creature can extemporize
with her dangling foot, richly decorated.
When she holds her hoard, proud of her rings
and naked, she bears her brothers on her neck –
a mighty kinswoman. Even a canny poet
will be hard put to name this creature.

32

This world is adorned in diverse ways,
decorated with rare ornaments.
I saw a strange contraption, an experienced traveller,
grind against the gravel and move away screaming.
This strange creature could not see; it had no shoulders,
arms, or hands; on one foot this oddity
journeys most rapidly, far over
the rolling sea. It has many ribs,
and a mouth in its middle, most useful to men.
It carried food in plenty, yielding tribute to all people
year by year, enjoyed by rich
and enjoyed by poor. Tell me if you can,
O man of wise words, what this creature is.

33

A curious, fair creature came floating on the waves,
shouting out to the distant shores,
resounding very loudly; her laughter was terrible
and fearsome to all. Sharp were her edges.
She is slow to join battle but severe in the fray,
smashing great ships with savagery.
She binds them with baleful charm,
and speaks with characteristic cunning:
'My mother, one of the beloved maidens,
is my daughter also, swollen and strong,
known by all people as she falls on the earth,
welcomed with love through the width of all lands.'

34

A strange object caught my eye, used to feed cattle
by men of every town; it has many teeth
and is useful to men as it scrapes around, its face
to the ground. It plunders greedily, searching for plants
along the grassy slopes, and brings them home;
it always finds those which are not rooted firmly,
but leaves the beautiful living flowers behind,
quietly standing where they spring from the soil,
brightly gleaming, blooming, growing.

35

The dank earth, wondrously cold,
first delivered me from her womb.
I know in my mind I wasn't made
from wool, skilfully fashioned with skeins.
Neither warp nor weft wind about me,
no thread thrums for me in the thrashing loom,
nor does a shuttle rattle for me,
nor does the weaver's rod bang and beat me.
Silkworms didn't spin with their strange craft for me,
those creatures that embroider cloth of gold.
Yet men will affirm all over this earth
that I'm an excellent garment.
O wise man, weigh your words
well, and say what this object is.

37

I saw a creature: his stomach stuck out behind him,
enormously swollen. A stalwart servant
waited upon him. What filled up his stomach
had travelled from far, and flew through his eye.
He does not always die in giving life
to others, but new strength revives
in the pit of his stomach; he breathes again.
He fathers a son; he's his own father also.

38

I saw a creature: masculine, greedy
with all youth's abandon, he guzzled
the four springs of what succoured him;
in sheer delight, he made them shoot out
gleaming. A man said to me:
'Alive, that creature breaks the downs;
dead and shredded, he binds the living.'

Books intimate that this creature has inhered
on middle-earth for aeons, evident
and plain to see. It has a pervasive power
far greater than people perceive. Its desire
is to seek out every living thing,
one by one; then it goes on its way.
It never spends two nights in the same place
but, homeless, follows forever the paths
of exile; no one despises it because of that.
It has neither hand nor foot, and never leaves
an imprint on the earth; no eyes either,
and no mouth, nor does it speak to men;
and it has no brain. But books explain
that this is the most swift creature
ever conceived in accordance with nature.
It lacks soul and life but must roam
far and wide throughout this wonderful world.
It lacks blood and bone yet benefits
many men throughout this middle-world.
It has never thrust to heaven, and never to hell,
but must exist always as the laws
of God decree. It would take long to tell
of how its life spins on, follows
fate's twisted pattern; that is a history
of marvels. Everything written
and told about this creature is true;
it has no offspring, it lives even so.
If you can give the answer quickly
and correctly, say what I am called.

Enduring the Creator, He who now guides
this earth on its foundations and governs this world.
Powerful is the Ruler, and properly King
and Sovereign over all; He governs and guides
earth and heaven, and they are encompassed by Him.
He made me – a marvel – at the Creation,
when He first fashioned this circle of earth;
He ordained that I should stay awake
and never sleep again, and sleep suddenly
overtakes me, my eyes quickly close.
In His authority the mighty Creator administers
this middle-earth in every respect;
so that I, at my Lord's leaving,
embrace this circle of earth entire.
I'm so timid that a drifting ghost
can frighten me terribly, and from end
to end I'm bolder than a wild boar
when, bristling with fury, it stands at bay;
no warrior on earth can overcome me,
but only God, who governs and guides
this high heaven. My fragrance
is much stronger than frankincense or rose
                    . . . grows in the greensward,
a delight; but I'm the more excellent;
although men love the lily of the field,
with its fair flower, I'm the finer;
likewise with my sweetness, always and everywhere,
I overpower the aroma of spikenard,
and I'm more foul than this murky fen

that, festering here, reeks of filth.
I govern one and all under the circle
of heaven for, at time's beginning, the beloved
Father bade me be impartial always
towards thick and thin; I assume everywhere
the form and feature of each thing.
I'm higher than heaven and God enjoins me
to keep to myself His mysterious nature;
I also see everything under the world,
the dismal pits of depraved spirits.
My age is much older than this circle of earth
or this middle-world could ever attain,
and I was born yesterday – a baby
from my mother's womb, acclaimed by men.
I'm more attractive than gold ornaments,
even if filigree work adorns them;
I'm more foul than this mouldering timber
or this slob of seaweed spewed up here.
I'm broader than the earth entire,
and more wide than this green world;
a hand can agitate me, and all that I am
can easily be held between three fingers.
I'm sharper and more biting than sharp frost,
the fierce rime that settles on the soil;
I'm hotter than the fire, the flames
surging and flickering at Vulcan's forge.
I am, besides, sweeter to the palate
than the honeycomb mingled with honey;
I'm more bitter than wormwood, too,
that stands, ashen, on this hillside.
I can gorge more greedily than an old giant,
holding my own in an eating match,
and I can always live content
if I see no food for as long as I live.

My flight is more powerful than the pernex,
the hawk or the eagle could ever aspire to;
no Zephyr – that restless breeze – ranges
as I do, rifling through every quarter;
the snail is swifter than I, the earthworm
more spry, and the fen frog outstrips me;
the offspring of dung (we call it
a weevil) crawls about more quickly.
I weigh much more than a grey boulder
or a hunk of lead, I'm much lighter
than this little insect that skitters
over the surface of the water with dry feet.
I'm tougher than flint, that strikes these sparks
from this adamant scrap of steel,
I'm much softer than this down, that here
in the wind wafts high into the air.
I'm broader than the earth entire
and more wide than this green world;
marvellously fashioned with miraculous skill,
I easily embrace all that lies beyond.
There is no kind of living creature in my care
to equal my power; I'm exalted
above every one of our Lord's creations,
Who alone, with His eternal might, can forcefully
stop me from swelling up. I'm more massive
and powerful than the huge whale who peers
dimly at the ocean bed, stronger than he
and yet I've less muscle than a mere tick
which sensible men dig out with a knife.
No white locks, delicately curled, cover
my head, but I'm bald all over;
nor do I have eyelids or lashes,
they were all cut off by the Creator;
now, lovely to see, curled locks

[62]

spring from my scalp, and grow until they
shine on my shoulders – an utter marvel.
I'm greater and more gross than the fattened pig,
the grunting hog, who lives happily
in the beech-wood, muddy and rooting,
so that he . . .

I watched a couple of curious creatures
copulating openly, out of doors;
the fair-haired one, flushed
beneath her garments, was filled with life
if that effort prospered. I can tell men
in the hall – those who are well-versed – the names
of these creatures with runes. There shall be
Need (N) twice over, and one gleaming
Ash (Æ) on the line, two Oaks (A)
and two Hails (H) also. With the key's power,
who has unlocked the treasury's chained door
that, firm in intent, denies runemen
access to the riddle, covered in its heart
with cunning bonds? Now they're exposed
to men drinking in the hall – the proper
names of this feather-brained pair.

43

I've heard tell of a noble guest;
man entertains him. He's not prey
to hunger pangs or burning thirst;
age and illness are unknown to him.
If the host serves him well, satisfies
this guest who must go on a journey,
both will be happy in their home,
live in prosperity, surrounded
by a family; but there'll be sorrow
if the host neglects his lordly guest,
his ruler on the journey. Think of them
as brothers, fearless of each other.
When they depart, together desert
one kinswoman (their mother and sister),
both suffer hurt. Let him who can
put names to the pair I describe –
the guest, then his servant, the host.

44

A strange thing hangs by man's hip,
hidden by a garment. It has a hole
in its head. It is stiff and strong
and its firm bearing reaps a reward.
When the retainer hitches his clothing
high above his knee, he wants the head
of that hanging thing to find the old hole
that it, outstretched, has often filled before.

45

I'm told a certain object grows
in the corner, rises and expands, throws up
a crust. A proud wife carried off
that boneless wonder, the daughter of a king
covered that swollen thing with a cloth.

46

A man sat sozzled with his two wives,
his two sons and his two daughters,
darling sisters, and with their two sons,
favoured firstborn; the father of that fine
pair was in there too, and so were
an uncle and a nephew. Five people
in all sat under that same roof.

47

A moth devoured words. When I heard
of that wonder it struck me as a strange event
that a worm should swallow the song of some man,
a thief gorge in the darkness on a great man's
speech of distinction. The thievish stranger
was not a whit the wiser for swallowing words.

48

I heard a radiant ring, with no tongue,
intercede for men, though it spoke
without argument or strident words.
The peaceful treasure pleaded for mankind:
'Heal me, save me, helper of souls.'
May men understand the mysterious saying
of the red gold and, as the ring said,
wisely entrust their salvation to God.

49

I know something that stands earthfast;
deaf and dumb, it often digests
useful gifts during the day handed over
by a servant. At times, in the houses of men,
some dark-skinned, swarthy slave
puts more into its mouth, dearer than gold,
things such as athelings, kings and queens,
dream of. But I will not name it,
this dumb creature here, this sombre nitwit,
that for their use gives back to brave men
exactly what it has eaten, earlier.

50

On earth there's a warrior of curious origin.
He's created, gleaming, by two dumb creatures
for the benefit of men. Foe bears him against foe
to inflict harm. Women often fetter him,
strong as he is. If maidens and men
care for him with due consideration
and feed him frequently, he'll faithfully obey them
and serve them well. Men succour him for the warmth
he offers in return; but this warrior will savage
anyone who permits him to become too proud.

51

I watched four fair creatures
travelling together; they left black tracks
behind them. The support of the bird
moved swiftly; it flew in the sky,
dived under the waves. The struggling warrior
continuously toiled, pointing out the paths
to all four over the fine gold.

52

I saw a couple of violent captives
carried in under the roof of the hall;
they were known by the same name,
tightly reined, fettered together.
Close to one stood a dark Welshman,
a slave to oversee the prisoners' movements.

53

I saw a tree towering in the wood
in vestments of bright green; the timber grew,
a joyous growth. Both water and earth
provided for it generously, but when it grew old
in times long ago, it was treated most terribly;
sorely wounded, and sullen in its chains,
its front was fettered with sombre trappings.
And now with brute force its butting-head
devastates, it opens the direct way
for a malicious enemy. In the mighty storm of battle
they often plunder the treasure hoard together.
Its butt is swift and restless whenever its head
runs the gauntlet for a comrade in distress.

54

A young man made for the corner
where he knew she was standing; this strapping churl
had walked some way – with his own hands
he whipped up her dress, and under her girdle
(as she stood there) thrust something stiff,
worked his will; they both shook.
This fellow quickened: one moment he was forceful,
a first-rate servant, so strenuous
that the next he was knocked up, quite
blown by his exertion. Beneath the girdle
a thing began to grow that upstanding men
often think of, tenderly, and acquire.

55

I saw in the hall (where visitors were drinking)
a wondrous tree, of four timbers, brought
on to the floor; it was adorned with twisted gold,
plated with silver, most skilfully inlaid
with jewels, a symbol of His cross who for us
established a ladder between Heaven and Earth
before He harrowed Hell. I can easily
tell you of this tree's origin:
the hard yew and shining holly,
the maple and the oak serve their Lord
together and together share one name –
an outlaw's tree it was that frequently offered
a weapon to its lord, a treasure in the hall,
the gold-hilted sword. Now tell me the answer
to this riddle, whoever will hazard
a guess as to what this tree is called.

56

I was in a room where I watched a piece
of wood, a shuttling beam, scathe
a struggling creature; it sustained battle-wounds,
savage gashes. Spears were the bane
of this creature, and with skill the beam
had been fixed securely. One of its feet
stood firm, the other strived busily,
pumped up and down, scraped the ground.
A tree stood there, near at hand, hung
with bright leaves. After spears had done their utmost,
I saw the leavings brought before my lord,
carried across the floor where warriors caroused.

57

This wind wafts little creatures
high over the hill-slopes. They are very
swarthy, clad in coats of black.
They travel here and there in hordes all together,
singing loudly, liberal with their songs.
Their haunts are wooded cliffs, yet they sometimes
come to the houses of men. They name themselves.

58

I know a creature in the field with one foot
and derring-do. It does not range widely
or ride very far, nor can it fly
through the bright air, or embark on some ship
with nailed sides; nonetheless
it obliges its master on many occasions.
It has a heavy tail and a little head,
a long tongue but not one tooth;
part of it is iron; it passes through a hole
in the earth. It eats nothing, drinks no water,
frets for no fodder, and yet often carries
liquid aloft. It boasts neither life
nor gifts from a lord, but still obeys
its owners. Three fitting runes
form its name: *Rad* is the first.

59

I watched men, wise in their minds,
and in their hearts serene, gaze at a golden
ring in the hall. God the saviour
has prayed for peace abounding for each guest
who turns the ring; then that ring spoke
a word to the gathering, it named the guardian
of virtuous men. Dumb as it was,
it clearly evoked the Maker's image
in the minds and eyes of anyone able
to understand the meaning of the marvellous gold
and the wounds of the Lord, and live as the wounds
of the ring ordained. Should the prayer
of any man be unfulfilled, his spirit
cannot enter the kingdom of God,
the castle of heaven. Let him who will
explain how the wounds of this wondrous ring
spoke to men when it was turned in the hall
and passed through proud retainers' hands.

60

I sank roots first of all, stood
near the shore, close by the dyke
and dash of waves; few men
saw my home in that solitary place,
but each dawn, each dusk,
dark waves surged around me, swirled
and made me sway. Little did I think
that I, mouthless, should ever sing
to men sitting at the mead-bench,
varying my pitch. It is very puzzling,
a miracle to men ignorant of such arts,
how a knife's point and a right hand
(mind and implement moving as one)
could cut and carve me – so that I
may send you a message without fear,
and so that no man in this wide world
will ever know what words we share.

61

A woman, young and lovely, often locked me
in a chest; she took me out at times,
lifted me with fair hands and gave me
to her loyal lord, fulfilling his desire.
Then he stuck his head well inside me,
pushed it upwards into the smallest part.
It was my fate, adorned as I was, to be filled
with something rough if that person who possessed me
was virile enough. Now guess what I mean.

62

I'm strong and pointed. Shuddering I die,
a violent release. For my reputable master
I'll plunge below the plimsoll line,
well and truly engineer an opening.
A desperate man stands behind me and develops me
himself; he carries a cloth. A southerner sometimes
helps me out of a hot spot (a real hole),
sometimes he gets me into a fix
and there quickly, quickly . . . What am I called?

65

Quick; quite mum; I die notwithstanding.
I lived once, I live again. Everybody
lifts me, grips me, and chops off my head,
bites my bare body, violates me.
I never bite a man unless he bites me;
there are many men who bite me.

66

I stretch beyond the bounds of the world,
I'm smaller than a worm, outstrip the sun,
I shine more brightly than the moon. The swelling seas,
the fair face of the earth and all the green fields,
are within my clasp. I cover the depths,
and plunge beneath hell; I ascend above heaven,
highland of renown; I reach beyond
the boundaries of the land of blessed angels.
I fill far and wide all the corners of the earth
and the ocean streams. Say what my name is.

69

On the way a miracle: water become bone.

70

This creature is odd, its habits unaccountable.
It sings through its sides. Its neck is curved,
skilfully carved, and above its back
it has pointed shoulders. It plays its fated part
as, gracefully, it stands by the roadside,
high and handsome, useful to men.

72

[*lines 1–5a defective*]

           . . . often I pulled at four
sweet brothers; each plied me
with drink day by day, it poured
through separate holes. I partook, contented,
until I was older and relinquished that
to the dark Welshman; I ranged further afield,
walked to the Welsh Marches, crossed the moors –
yoked under a beam, with a ring round my neck,
such drudgery dogged me step by step,
a share of hardship. Often the iron
gashed my sides grievously; I kept
quiet, never complained to any man
if the spear-stabs were painful.

74

I was once a young woman,
a glorious warrior, a grey-haired queen.
I soared with birds, stepped on the earth,
swam in the sea – dived under waves,
dead amongst fishes. I had a living spirit.

76

I saw a woman, solitary, brooding.

77

The deep sea suckled me, the waves sounded over me;
rollers were my coverlet as I rested on my bed.
I have no feet and frequently open my mouth
to the flood. Sooner or later some man will
consume me, who cares nothing for my shell.
With the point of his knife he will pierce me through,
ripping the skin away from my side, and straight away
eat me uncooked as I am . . .

80

I'm loved by my lord, and his shoulder
companion, I'm the comrade of a warrior,
a friend of the King. Frequently the fair-haired
Queen, the daughter of an earl, deigns
to lay her hand upon me in spite of her nobility.
I carry within me what grew in the grove.
Sometimes I ride on a proud steed
at the head of the host; harsh is my voice.
Very often I recompense the gleeman
for his songs. I'm sombre in colour,
and kind at heart. What am I called?

81

My breast is puffed up and my neck is swollen.
I've a fine head and a high waving tail,
ears and eyes also but only one foot;
a long neck, a strong beak, a back and
two sides, and a rod right through my middle.
My home is high above men. When he who moves
the forest molests me, I suffer a great deal of misery.
Scourged by the rainlash, I stand alone;
I'm bruised by heavy batteries of hail,
Hoar-frost attacks and snow half-hides me.
I must endure all this, not pour out my misery.

83

My origin was age-old [I endured many winters];
I lived in towns after the keeper of fire
[unlocked the lives] of men encircled by flame,
purged by fire. Now the brother of earth,
my enemy, who from the first brought me
misfortune, imprisons me. I well remember
who drew me and my like from our first
abode; I can do him no evil
but at times I'm an instrument of bondage
the whole world over. I've many talents,
on middle-earth I've vast strength,
but I must conceal from all men
the mysterious source of my precious skill
and my extraction. Guess what I'm called.

84

On earth there's a creature wondrously conceived:
she's wild and unruly, unbridled her momentum;
ferociously she roars as she rolls across the earth.
She has mothered many splendid creatures.
This fair traveller is eager always,
headstrong and inescapable. No one can find
words appropriate to describe to others
her splendid appearance, her innumerable kin,
her ancient origin; the Father saw it all,
the beginning and end, and so did the Son,
sublime child of the Creator . . .
[*lines 11b–20 defective or missing*]
This mother is endowed with massive strength;
wondrously sustained, teeming with food
and treasure-adorned, she's dear to men.
Her force increases, her might is revealed,
her grace is enhanced by the great good she offers –
a gift refreshing for proud people,
she's pure and bountiful, boundless her excellence.
She's precious to the rich, useful to the poor,
priceless and freeborn; of all things created
under the sky, on which the sons of men
have set eyes, she's the strongest,
the most strenuous as she covers the ground,
the most grasping and most greedy (so lives
this glorious creature, kinswoman of mortals),
although keen in mind . . .
a more discerning man, a host of marvels.
She's harder than earth, older than heroes,

more generous than gold-givers, dearer than gems;
she beautifies the world, gives birth
to plants, washes away suffering.
From outside, she casts a veil –
a marvellous making – over countless people,
and on earth everywhere men gaze in wonder . . .
[lines 43–56 *defective*]

85

My abode's by no means silent,
but I am not loud-mouthed.
The Lord Almighty laid down laws
for both of us together – I'm swifter
than he who harbours me and sometimes
stronger too, he must strive more laboriously.
At times I quietly rest, while he must run onward.
But I live in him all the days of my life;
if we're ever divided, my destiny is death.

86

A creature came shuffling where there sat
many wise men in the meeting-place.
He had two ears and only one eye,
he had two feet and twelve hundred heads,
a back, two hands, and a belly,
two shoulders and sides, a neck,
and two arms. Now tell me his name.

91

My head was hammered into shape, scarred
by sharp chisels, scoured by a file.
I swallow what faces me whenever,
wearing rings, I thrust firmly
against a hard object; hollowed out
from behind, I strain at what stands
between my lord and his mind's desire
at midnight. I guard gold at times,
and pull back my poking nose
when my lord plans to plunder heirlooms
from those he has subdued, to wreak
savage vengeance just as he pleases.

[*lines* 1–8 *defective*]
At times he would spring up the steep slopes
in his own fells, then at times plunge
into deep dales, with great leaps,
in search of food; he kicked up frozen
scree, sometimes he shook the frost
from his ashen hair.

                  With the eager ones I rode
until my younger brother usurped my position
(happy it was) and drove me from my home.
After that an iron weapon, gleaming,
gashed my stomach; although the sharp-edged steel
bit into me savagely, no blood, no gore,
issued from me. I did not mourn that hour
nor weep at my wound, nor was I able
to avenge my misfortune with a warrior's life;
rather, I suffer pain from all those
that have bitten the shield. Now I swallow black –
wood and water – and in my womb incorporate
something dark that (as I stand here)
falls on me from above; I have one foot.
Now the preying enemy, who once bore the wolf's companion
far and wide, pilfers my treasure;
it often sallies out of my stomach,
adorns the stout table . . .
[*lines* 32*b*–35 *defective*]

95

I'm a noble object known to warriors,
and often quietly rest; renowned amongst
high and humble, I range far and wide
and plunderers' pickings are mine if I,
once remote from friends, can but win
success and shining reward in halls.
Now discerning men appreciate
my presence; I'll reveal wisdom
to many people, all over the earth
they fall silent. Although the sons of men,
livers on land, watch eagerly now
for some sign of me. I sometimes
conceal my tracks from all humankind.

NOTES

Riddle 1

The *Exeter Book* riddles begin with a dramatic description of a storm. There has been much discussion as to whether lines 1–74 constitute one, two or three riddles; but the scribe has divided his material into three parts, and I have elected to follow him. The invitation in the closing lines of Riddles 1 and 2 follows a convention often used to round off the riddles, and strongly suggests that we are dealing with three separate entities, but on the other hand the last paragraph of Riddle 3 appears to be a recapitulation of all that has gone before. The solution to this first riddle is generally taken to be *storm on land*, but this and the following two riddles are not really enigmatic; they are fine descriptive poems. Lines 12–14 refer to the Old Testament Flood.

Riddle 2

Commentators have accepted that the answer to this riddle (or part of a riddle) is *submarine earthquake*. It could, however, be *storm at sea*. The first part of Riddle 3 describes an earthquake on land, while Riddle 1 describes a storm on land: these sandwiched lines look in both directions.

Riddle 3

These forceful lines describe an earthquake, a storm at sea, and a thunderstorm back on land. The most sensible blanket designation is *storm*. The word 'shrithing' in line 50 derives from the Old English *scripan*, meaning a sinewy and sinister thrusting movement; it is also used by the *Beowulf*-poet in describing both the monster Grendel and the dragon. The Anglo-Saxons' love and fear of the sea is conveyed as well in these lines as anywhere in Old English literature. The 'flint-grey rollers', the 'spines of breakers' and the 'yells of sailors' are the phrases of a man who has really visualized these things and knows how to describe them.

Riddle 4

Millstone, *flail* and *lock* have their advocates, but *bell* is the most favoured solution to this riddle. Cathedrals and leading churches in Anglo-Saxon England may not have boasted teams of campanologists but they were certainly equipped with a bell or bells: a page from the tenth-century *Benedictional of St Æthelwold* shows the Saint blessing a congregation from the door of the new cathedral at Winchester which he had rebuilt in 980, and the cathedral is furbished with a splendid bell-tower with three bells; and it is crowned with a weathercock (see Riddle 81). This riddle may point to the secular use of bells.

Riddle 5

Shield. The rune for S, which can represent either *scyld* or *scutum* (shield) is written beneath this riddle, the first of several in the *Exeter Book* concerned with weaponry. The circular or kite-shaped curved shield of wood, covered with hide with an iron boss, was the most common weapon of defence. Nothing portrays as vividly as the Bayeux Tapestry the way in which the shield stood – or failed to stand – between man and sword, man and axe, and, as the *Beowulf*-poet says, man and 'the iron-tipped arrow-shower'.

Riddle 6

Sun. As a kind of extra clue, the same rune that closes Riddle 5 closes this riddle too; in this instance it is thought to represent either *sigel* or *sol* (sun). No matter what the riddler says, Anglo-Saxon summers were not tropical, but much of a muchness with those we experience today.

Riddle 7

Swan. This riddle touches on the classical tradition that the swan has musical plumage, in that harmony and sweetness are produced by the breath of the West wind against its wings. And most musically it begins:

> Hraegl min swigeð, þonne ic hrusan trede,
> oþþe pa wic buge, oþþe wado drefe.

These and the following lines (the first that I translated from Old English, having just been attacked by a swan) foreshadow that great poem by W. B. Yeats, 'The Wild Swans at Coole':

> But now they drift on the still water,
> Mysterious, beautiful;
> Among what rushes will they build,
> By what lake's edge or pool
> Delight man's eyes when I awake some day
> To find they have flown away?

Riddle 8

Commentators dispute the answer to this riddle with the voices of Babel: *nightingale, wood-pigeon, chough, jackdaw, bell* (most unconvincingly) have been suggested, but *jay*, first proposed by Frederick Tupper, seems the most likely solution. This riddle and Riddle 24 (which contains its own answer, *higora* – jay or magpie) have much in common. I find the picture of men at the day's end who 'sit, bowed down, quiet in their houses' moving in its contrast to the songbird's unabashed vigour.

Riddle 9

Cuckoo. Here is the familiar, cruel story of the fledgling cuckoo, told in a charming way. There are several references to the bird in Old English literature, capitalizing on the paradox that its two-toned song was the melancholy announcement of something gay, as, for example, in 'The Seafarer':

> And the cuckoo, harbinger of summer, sings
> a mournful song, boding bitter sorrow
> to the heart . ...

Riddle 10

Speculation that the answer to this riddle might be *ocean-furrow* or *bubble* or *anchor* or *water-lily* have given way to a consensus that the right solution is *barnacle goose*, first proposed by Stopford Brooke in his *History of Early English Literature*. The barnacle goose (*Anas leucopsis*), a species of wild goose that breeds in the Arctic and visits Britain in winter, was once thought to be produced out of a barnacle shell, while another school of thought held that barnacle geese grew on trees, to which they were attached by their bills. In the twelfth century Giraldus Cambrensis noted:

Bernacae are like marsh-geese, but somewhat smaller. They are produced from fir-timber tossed along the sea, and are at first like gum. Afterwards they hang down by their beaks, as if from a seaweed attached to the timber, surrounded by shells in order to grow more freely. Having thus in process of time been clothed with a strong coat of feathers, they either fall into the water or fly freely away into the air.

Riddle 11

Four solutions, *wine, beaker of wine, night* and *gold*, have been proposed. The internal evidence of the poem (especially lines 5b–8) and the similarities to Riddle 27 (*mead*) make *wine* the most likely. The crucial penultimate line appears to have been wrongly copied by the *Exeter Book* scribe and has provoked much argument: a small emendation enables one to translate it as I have done, in which case the 'dearest of hoards' may refer to the soul; a larger emendation allows the literal translation, 'when the dearest of hoards (the sun) hastens on high', leading to the solution *night*.

The Anglo-Saxons drank mead and ale day-in, day-out, and there are many references to both drinks in their literature. Wine was a rarer commodity and a pupil in Ælfric's *Colloquy*, a dialogue used in monastery schools to teach Latin, comments, 'I'm not rich enough to buy myself wine; and wine isn't a drink for children or the foolish, but for the old and wise.' There were some vineyards in the South of England and much wine was imported from France and Germany in large *amphorae* and in wooden barrels like those depicted in the Bayeux Tapestry. When the merchant in the same *Colloquy* is asked what he brings to England, he replies: 'Purple garments and silks; precious gems and gold, strange raiment and spice; wine and oil; ivory and brass; copper and tin; sulphur and glass, and many such things . . .'

Riddle 12

Leather, depicted first on the living ox, then made into thongs, into a gourd, and into shoes. There are analogues in the four Latin riddle collections with which the *Exeter Book* riddler was familiar. In particular, the last two lines are very close to the end of Eusebius' Riddle 37 (*calf*): 'And if I live, I begin to plough up hills; or if I die, I bind up many who are alive.' The

Old English word *wealh* (lines 3 and 7) means 'Welshman', 'Cornishman', 'slave' and 'shameless one' – a reflection of the old bitter conflict between Celt and Saxon in the fifth and sixth centuries, when many Britons were taken into slavery. Consider the wars of the Middle Ages, the long tormented history of Ireland, the self-government of Man, the present nationalist parties and policies; in many ways, the struggle still continues. In the words of R. S. Thomas:

> We are not English . . . *Ni bydd diwedd*
> *Byth ar sŵn y delyn aur.*
> Though the strings are broken, and time sets
> The barbed wire in their place,
> The tune endures; on the cracked screen
> Of life our shadows are larger still
> In history's fierce afterglow.

(Lines from 'Border Blues' in *Poetry for Supper*, Hart-Davis, London, 1958. The Welsh words mean, 'There will never be an end to the sound of the golden harp.')

Riddle 13

The solution *ten chickens* is widely but not universally accepted. Mrs van Erhardt-Siebold explains the six brothers and their sisters by pointing out that in Old English ten chickens, *ten ciccenu*, has six consonants and four vowels. When it is hatched, a chicken leaves its membrane clinging to the inside of the shell.

Riddle 14

Horn. This is the more elaborate and perhaps less poetically satisfying of the two 'horn' riddles (the other is Riddle 80) in the *Exeter Book*. The horn lived first on the head of the aurochs or wild ox. Great herds once roamed through the forests of north-west Europe but the animal became extinct five or six hundred years ago. Then the horn was decorated and used to hold wine (on average, it held three to four pints), or to summon men to battle.

Riddle 15

Badger is the most widely accepted solution, although a case has also been made out for *porcupine* (known to Anglo-Saxons as *se mara igil*, 'the larger hedgehog'), *fox* and *hedgehog*. There are many textual difficulties and, consequently, opportunities for different interpretation. Stopford Brooke observed: 'It is in these short poems – in this sympathetic treatment of the beasts of the wood, as afterwards of the birds; in this transference to them of human passions and of the interest awakened by their suffering and pleasure – that the English poetry of animals begins.'

Riddle 16

Anchor. This riddle is an elaboration of Symphosius' Riddle 61 (*anchor*): 'My twin points are joined by a single bar of iron. I struggle with the wind; I fight with the deep sea. I probe into the middle of the waters; I also bite the earth itself.'

Riddle 17

Ballista, *fortress* and *oven* have been advocated as solutions; the similarities between this riddle and Riddle 23, which declares itself to be a bow, make *ballista* the most likely solution. Used by Greeks, Romans and many other early cultures, the *ballista* is 'an ancient military engine, resembling a bow stretched with cord and thongs, used to hurl stones, etc.'.

Riddle 18

I'm a strange creature; I can't speak a word,
amuse men with talk, although I've a mouth,
a massive paunch . . .

*

I was on a ship surrounded by my family.

These three and a half lines are all that survive of what must have been a longer riddle, although no loss is indicated in the manuscript. The last line appears to belong to some other riddle. One commentator, Dietrich, has volunteered *leather bottle* as a solution; he may be right, but it is worth noting the object in question has the same 'massive paunch' ascribed to *bellows* in Riddles 37 and 87.

Riddle 19

On my way I saw S R O
H so spirited, with gleaming mane,
galloping hard across the green plain.
On its back it bore battle-might;
N O M without a weapon rode
A G E W. Ranging far, fleet of foot
on its journey, it carried a keen C O
F O A H. The way, the track of these travellers
was the more noble. Guess my name.

This riddle is dominated by four runic groups which read SROH, NOM, AGEW (probably) and COFOAH. Read backwards, we have the Old English words *hors*, *mon*, *wega* and *haofoc* – 'horse', 'man', 'ways', and 'hawk'. It is impossible to say more than that this riddle, and its companion Riddle 64, revolve around these four constituents; there does not appear to be an answer as such. Since the riddle seems too generalized to refer to some specific story, it was more probably just a poet's test as to whether his audience were good *rynemenn*, 'runemen'.

Riddle 20

Sword is accepted by all commentators save one who takes the solution to be *hawk* or *falcon*. The riddle is incomplete, and Krapp and Dobbie, editors of *The Anglo-Saxon Poetic Records*, comment that 'the evidence of the gatherings reinforces the evidence of the text that a folio has been lost at this point, containing the remainder of Riddle 20 and probably some other riddles as well.' The conflict between the beautiful, chaste sword and the scold, resentful at her husband's lack of attention, is vivid and amusing, and it is a pity that only part of it survives.

To own a sword implied standing and wealth; maybe it was the mark of a thane. The most renowned of swords were important bequeathals (King Alfred mentions one in his will) and had lineages of famous owners; they also had names, such as 'Nægling', Beowulf's sword, which snapped in his fight against the dragon. The blades, almost a metre long, were sometimes engraved with ornamental patterning or with runes, like the sword found at Lincoln bearing the mysterious music ANTANANANTANANTAN, but the finest decoration (as this riddle indicates) was usually reserved for the hilt.

Riddle 21

Plough. The 'grey foe of the forest' could be either iron (which, as an axe, felled a tree) or, possibly, the ploughman. The two sharp weapons are the share and coulter. The passage about the lot of the ploughman in Ælfric's *Colloquy* is charming and moving:

PLOUGHMAN: O Master, I work very hard; I go out at dawn, drive the oxen to the field, and yoke them to the plough. There is no storm so severe that I dare to hide at home, for fear of my lord, but when the oxen are yoked, and the share and coulter have been fastened to the plough, I must plough a whole acre or more every day.

TEACHER: Have you any companion?

PLOUGHMAN: I have a boy to urge on the oxen with a goad; he is now hoarse on account of the cold and his shouting.

TEACHER: What else do you do during the day?

PLOUGHMAN: I do a great deal more. I must fill the bins of the oxen with the hay, water them, and carry off their dung.

TEACHER: Oh! Oh! The labour must be great.

PLOUGHMAN: It is indeed great drudgery, because I am not free.

Riddle 22

Although some commentators believe that the answer to this riddle is *the circling stars* (or the Great Bear or Charles's Wain), and cite Aldhelm's riddle 'Arcturus' as a remote analogue, the evidence in favour of the solution, *the month of December*, seems to me to be conclusive. The 'sixty men' are the sixty half-days, or days and nights, of the month – there are many examples of the Anglo-Saxons' habit of counting in halves. The eleven men mounted on 'horses of peace' are the month's four Sundays and seven feast days (Conception of the Virgin, St Nicholas, St Thomas, Christmas, St Stephen, St John Evangelist, Holy Innocents). The water divides one year from the next and the 'opposite side' is therefore January. These ramifications are rather elaborate, but see the Introduction (p. 8) for a discussion of the Time-Riddle.

Riddle 23

Bow. The first word of the riddle is *agof* which, read backwards, gives *foga* which is an earlier form of *boga*, bow. The archer was by no means a commonplace of Anglo-Saxon warfare. Indeed it was essentially the massed archers and cavalry who enabled the Normans to scrape home at Hastings.

Riddle 24

Jay, magpie. The runes in this riddle read G, Æ, R, O, H and I. This is an anagram of *higoræ* (= *higore*), which is the feminine form of *higora*, jay or magpie. These lines abound with onomatopoeia: the dog *beorce*, barks; the goat *blaete*, bleats; the goose *graede*, honks; and the hawk *gielle* (pronounced 'yella'), shrieks.

Riddle 25

The seven 'obscene' riddles in the *Exeter Book* have embarrassed most commentators, who have gone to considerable lengths not to face facts. In this instance, however, the Anglo-Saxon riddler has been sufficiently ambiguous to save their faces. The ostensible-answer is *onion* (other suggestions have been *leek*, *hip* – fruit of the wild rose – *hemp* and *mustard*) and the innuendo-answer is *penis*. Apart from its success as *double entendre*, this and the other 'obscene' riddles show the Anglo-Saxon sense of humour to have been not only ironic (as many Old English poems demonstrate) but, as one might expect, earthy. It is worth reiterating that the *Exeter Book* was compiled for a bishop to donate to his cathedral library. Pious and ascetic the Anglo-Saxon monks were but, unlike some contemporary critics, they were not prim.

Riddle 26

Book, clearly religious, maybe a copy of the Gospels. The *Exeter Book* riddler was plainly aware of, but did not imitate, Aldhelm's Riddles 32 and 59 (*writing-tablets* and *quill*) and Eusebius' Riddles 32 and 33 (*parchment* and *quill*).

The production of a book before the revolutionary invention of the printing press – surely the most significant invention of all time – was a lengthy business. Each monastery had its own scriptorium and, especially during the seventh and eighth centuries, Anglo-Saxon monasteries produced a steady stream of books – copies of the scriptures, biblical exegeses, treatises on grammar, natural science, chronology, lives of the saints, and so forth – for use at home and abroad. A touching letter from Abbot Cuthbert of Wearmouth in 773 to a continental bishop who had asked for copies of Bede's works has something to say about the scribe's working conditions: 'And if I could have done more, I would gladly have done so. For the conditions of the past winter oppressed the island of our race very horribly with cold and ice and long and widespread storms of wind and rain, so that the hand of the scribe was hindered from producing a great number of books.'

The Roman Catholic church has always maintained that no expense or effort should be spared over objects made to the greater glory of God, and there are few greater glories than the best Anglo-Saxon illuminated manuscripts, such as the *Lindisfarne Gospels*. Far from simply acting as copyists, the ascetic monks decorated their functional manuscripts inside and out with a grand, controlled passion; the vellum pages, glowing with solid mineral colours, red lead, bluish green (extracted from malachite), bright yellow (extracted from arsenic salts), and pink, blue, purple, brown and gold, are works of art of the very highest order.

This riddle occupies an extraordinary place in our literature. It was composed to be recited, and yet it celebrates something that is read. It stands at the crossroads of the oral and written traditions.

Riddle 27

Mead. A thane's wife was responsible for the brewing of ale and the making of mead, which consists of water and fermented honey and was stored in urns. It is extremely strong but rather sickly, and was doubtless diluted. Honey was the only form of sweetening known to the Anglo-Saxons and consequently bees and the art of bee-keeping were highly prized. A charm survives, words once spoken to restrain bees:

> *When they swarm, scatter earth over them and say*:
> 'Alight, victorious women, alight on the earth!
> Never turn wild and fly to the woods!
> Be just as mindful of my benefit
> As is every man of his food and fatherland.'

Riddle 28

Although some commentators have proposed *wine-cask* and *harp*, the evidence is overwhelmingly in favour of *John Barleycorn* or *ale*. In making my translation I have leant heavily on John Seymour's admirable description of the process of harvesting and malting barley and making ale (fermented malt) in *The Complete Book of Self-Sufficiency* (Faber, 1976). My version of lines 4–6 to some extent simplifies the original – but then a word like 'sparging' is not common coin in the way its equivalent was to the Anglo-Saxons. There is unfortunately no way is which a translator can echo the remarkable music (achieved by adding rhyming pairs to the usual alliteration and four-stress line) of this same passage:

> corfen, sworfen,   cyrred, þyrred,
> bunden, wunden,   blaeced, waeced,
> fraetwed, geatwed,   feorran laeded
> to durum dryhta

Riddle 29

Moon and sun is widely accepted, although a case has also been made out for *swallow and sparrow*, *bird and wind* and *cloud and wind*. The concept that the moon has horns and plunders the sun's light has the quality and weight of myth; this seems to me a most successful riddle and an appropriately mysterious and haunting poem.

Riddle 30a

For some reason there are two widely separated, virtually identical texts of Riddle 30 in the *Exeter Book*. I have followed the example of Krapp and Dobbie in *The Anglo-Saxon Poetic Records* in designating them Riddles 30a and 30b. (Riddle 30b follows Riddle 59.) There has been much discussion as to the composite parts of the solution, but it is agreed that the riddle is a pun on the Old English word *beam*, which carried a number of meanings. The meaning 'tree' suits lines 1b–2 and 3b–4a; the meaning 'ship' fits line 3a, 'log' lines 1a and 4b, and 'cup' lines 5–6. In the last three lines Christ's Cross (*beam* also means wood) speaks in the first person, as it does in the finest of the Old English religious poems, 'The Dream of the Rood'.

Riddle 31

Bagpipe is almost universally accepted. In this charming and effective portrayal of the instrument as a rather helpless, dumb bird who can only 'extemporize with her dangling foot', the beak is the chanter and the brothers are the drones. Paradoxically, the hoard in line 20 consists of nothing but air, with which the bag is inflated. Writing in the sixth century, Procopius refers to the bagpipe as the war instrument of Roman infantry. Horn and harp often appear in manuscript illumination and poem, and remains of them have been unearthed in archaeological discoveries – perhaps there were as few Anglo-Saxons unable to pick up a stringed instrument and recite a poem as there are people in Britain and America today unable to read – but references to other musical instruments are infrequent.

Riddle 32

Probably *ship*. *Wheel*, *millstone* and *wagon* have also been suggested. Krapp and Dobbie comment that 'the vessel described in the riddle is one of the decked merchant ships of the late Anglo-Saxon period, the *muð*, line 9, being the hatchway.'

Riddle 33

Iceberg. The riddler was probably working on hearsay, for icebergs were seen no further south than they are today. In *The Art of Poesie* (1589), Puttenham wrote:

We dissemble again under covert and dark speeches, when we speak by way of riddle (*Enigma*) of which the sense can hardly be picked out, but by the parties owne assoile, as he that said:

'It is my mother well I wot
And yet the daughter that I begot!'.

Meaning by it the ise which is made of frozen water, the same, being molten by the sunne or fire, makes water again.

Riddle 34

Rake. The object described is mundane but the treatment is sensitive and the atmospheric ending unforced.

Riddle 35

Coat of mail. This is quite a close translation of Aldhelm's Riddle 33; and at the end of a collection of Aldhelm's riddles in Leiden University Library there is another version of this riddle, written in Northumbrian dialect. The device of solution by elimination makes for a most effective riddle.

Riddle 36

I saw a creature riding over the rollers,
its adornments were distinctive and strange.
It had four feet beneath its stomach
and eight –
man . hwm . woman . mxlkfwf . horse . qxxs .
      – on its back;
it had two wings, twelve eyes,
and six heads. Say what it was.
It surged over the swell; and it was not
a bird alone, for it bore the likeness
of a horse, a man and a hound, also
the shape of a woman. You who are able
to ascertain the answer can spell out
this creature's name, and explain its nature.

'This is one of the riddles', wrote A. J. Wyatt, 'one wishes at the bottom of the Bay of Portugal: there is no poetry in it, and the ingenuity is misplaced.' *Ship* is commonly accepted as the solution, but this should really be extended to *a ship with three passengers* or some such if lines 7–12 are taken into account. Interpretations of these lines differ: perhaps Frederick Tupper's argument is the most convincing – namely, that the four feet are oars and the eight 'on its back' are the feet of the man, woman and horse on deck. He continues, 'The horse, man, dog, bird, and woman, of which it bears the likeness (ie. which it carries), supply, if we add the ship's figurehead, the two wings, twelve eyes, and six heads.'

It is thought that line 5 was a marginal note and not originally part of the riddle; it is not as complicated as it looks, but is simply written in a code in which each vowel is represented by the consonant in the alphabet that follows it. The scribe, however, has slipped up and both miscopied and misplaced the cryptic lettering, which, decoded, should actually read, *homo*, *mulier* and *equus*, each repeating the Old English word that precedes it.

Riddle 37

This is one of two riddles (the other is Riddle 87) to which the answer is *bellows*, and with a certain amount of *double entendre* it wittily develops Symphosius' Riddle 73, which reads: 'I do not die immediately when the breath leaves, for it returns continually; although it often departs again too. At one time my soul's power is considerable; at another, it is nothing.' The last line means that the bellows gives birth to air (as it pumps it out), yet also gives itself air and life (as it draws air in).

Riddle 38

Young bull. The bullock drinks at its mother's four teats. Alive, it breaks ground with the plough; dead, its hide forms thongs. Traditionally, it was with a thong that Hengest (a Saxon mercenary) first established himself in England after Vortigern had asked for his assistance. In the words of that unreliable twelfth-century historian Geoffrey of Monmouth, Hengest says: 'Grant me, then, as much land as can be encircled by a thong.' Vortigern agrees and Hengest 'then took the hide of a bull and cut it into a single leather thong. With this thong he marked out a certain precipitous site, which he had chosen with the greatest possible cunning. Inside the space which he had measured he began to build a fortress.'

Riddle 39

Time, *day* and *moon* have been proposed, but line 20, 'It has never thrust to heaven', appears to rule out *moon*. In line 14 I have taken the emendation *earuvost*, 'most swift', which makes better sense than *earmost*, 'most wretched'. The language of this riddle is rather impoverished and also seems to me rather long-winded.

Riddle 40

Creation. This is much the longest riddle in the collection and, even so, it is incomplete because a leaf is missing between folios 111 and 112 of the *Exeter Book*. It is a translation of Aldhelm's Riddle 100, *De Creatura*. Paull F. Baum notes that the Anglo-Saxon poet generally needed two lines for each hexameter and adds: 'This use of two lines for one is responsible for the thinness of the style.' It is true that there are some limp lines, some *longueurs* and some difficulties with the Latin (though few translators will think it wise to rail at another's rare howler!), notably the invention of the 'pernex' in line 66, where the poet misunderstood *plus pernex aquilis* ('swifter than the eagle') and took the adjective to be the name of a bird; but this riddle is also packed out with memorable images and vivid contrasts, and at times achieves a degree of real authority.

Riddle 41

Only the last eight and a half lines of the riddle survive; it began on the missing folio (see note to Riddle 40). No translation is offered because these lines provide no basis for a solution and are of little poetic consequence. They refer to an object which is the mother of many children, who are the 'best' and 'darkest' and 'dearest' owned by men, and say that we must 'enjoy what the children of men do' if we are to live on earth at all. *Wisdom* and three of the elements – *earth*, *fire* and *water* – have been tentatively advanced as answers.

Riddle 42

Cock and hen. Rearranged, the runes read *hana*, 'cock', and *hæn*, 'hen'. Lines 10b to 14a are rather involved; the poet was perhaps straining too hard after effects.

Riddle 43

Soul and body. The 'noble guest' is the soul; its servant and brother is the body. The earth is mother and sister to them both – mother because man's body is made of dust, and sister because she was made by the same father, God. The nature and relationship of the soul and body is also the subject of several longer Anglo-Saxon texts.

Riddle 44

Most leading commentators accept the ostensible-answer *key*, but the innuendo-answer is obviously *penis*. The first lines are promisingly suggestive, but overall this riddle is not sufficiently ambiguous (see note to Riddle 25) to avoid crudity.

Riddle 45

Dough, leavened with an ounce or two of *double entendre.*

Riddle 46

Lot with his two daughters and their sons. Genesis 19: 30–38 tells how Lot feared to live in Zoar and went to live with his profligate daughters in a mountain cave; there they twice made him drunk and each seduced him. 'Thus were both the daughters of Lot with child by their father.' One bore Moab, and the other Ben-ammi. The first use of this incestuous story for the purposes of a riddle is attributed to the Queen of Sheba; she tried it on Solomon.

Riddle 47

Bookmoth. The source for these charming lines is Symphosius' Riddle 16, 'Tinea': 'Writing has fed me, but I don't know what writing is. I have lived in books, but am no more learned because of it. I have consumed the Muses, yet up till now I have not improved myself.'

Riddle 48

The answer to this riddle is some kind of church plate: either *chrismal*, *paten* or *chalice*. It has similarities to Riddle 59. The Romans mined gold, famous for its red lustre, at Dolaucothi in Carmarthenshire, and there has recently been talk of re-opening this mine. It sounds as if this object was fashioned from ore from the same source. Many Anglo-Saxon gold objects were made from melted and re-cycled Roman coins.

Riddle 49

Book-case is held to be the most likely solution, but *falcon-cage* and *oven* have also been suggested; Aldhelm's Riddle 89 has been cited as an analogue. Very few individuals would have possessed books of their own, let alone the 'twenty book, clad in blak or reed' later preferred by Chaucer's Clerk of Oxenford; most manuscripts belonged to the monasteries where they were written, illuminated and bound (see note to Riddle 26), or else to cathedral libraries.

Riddle 50

Most critics accept the solution *fire*. The 'two dumb creatures' must be flints, or pieces of steel, or even possibly pieces of wood.

Riddle *51*

Pen and three fingers is widely accepted, in which case the 'four fair creatures' can be explained as the thumb, three fingers and pen, a quill which as a feather had once supported the swift bird; the 'struggling warrior' would be the arm of the scribe; and the 'gold' may refer to manuscript illumination or possibly to inlay on the ink-horn (subject of Riddles 88 and 93). Less convincing cases have also been made out for the solutions *dragon* and *horse and waggon*.

The *Exeter Book* itself is written in a generous, attractive hand and is generally supposed to be the work of one scribe. Krapp and Dobbie note: 'The variations which we find in the writing of the *Exeter Book* are by no means too great to be explained as a result of variations in the quality of the parchment and the use of different pens.'

Riddle *52*

The commonly accepted solution is *flail*, although *well-buckets* and *a yoke of oxen led into a barn by a female slave* and *broom* have had their advocates. The two 'violent captives' can be interpreted as the flail's handle and swingle.

Riddle *53*

Battering ram. The Anglo-Saxons were very conscious of the power and beauty of trees, and of their use and abuse by men. The *lance* (Riddle 73) alludes to fierce foes that first cut it down when it was a tree; the *bow* (Riddle 23) refers to its torment; and the *plough* (Riddle 21) speaks of its many scars. And, in 'The Dream of the Rood', the tree hewn into the Cross says:

> 'I remember the morning a long time ago
> that I was felled at the edge of the forest

and severed from my roots. Strong enemies
seized me and fashioned me for their sport,
bade me hold up their felons on high.'

Riddle 54

This is one of the more witty and successful of the *double
entendre* riddles. A nice balance is struck between the ostensible-
answer, *churn*, and the innuendo-answer which could perhaps
be designated *coition*.

Riddle 55

The editors of *The Anglo-Saxon Poetic Records* put paid to
shield, *scabbard*, *gallows*, *cross* and *harp*, and demonstrate that
sword-rack must be the solution. The object is portayed in the
shape of both cross and gallows, and is made of four kinds of
timber as the Cross was often said to have been. The paradox
of the tree that is decorated with gold, silver and jewels and
that causes suffering and death is developed more fully in
'The Dream of the Rood' (see notes to Riddles 30a and 53).

Riddle 56

Probably *loom*. The 'struggling creature' is the web and the
'spears' have been explained by Mrs von Erhardt-Siebold as
'the teeth of a batten penetrating through the warp'. The
'bright leaves' probably refer to flax on a distaff.

Riddle 57

There is now general agreement that the solution is likely to
be some species of bird (thereby disposing of the earlier
proposals, *hail-stones*, *rain-drops* and *gnats*), but it is impossible

to say which. *Swallows, starlings, jackdaws* and *crows* have been advocated, and it seems to me that the internal evidence of the poem also makes *house-martins* a possibility. There is a charming springy lift to the original, which begins:

> þeos lyft byreð   lytle wihte
> ofer beorghleoþa.   þa sind blace swiþe,
> swearte salopade.

Riddle 58

Draw-well is the commonly accepted answer to this riddle, but these lines in fact describe only the *well-sweep* – the long pole attached to an upright, with a bucket hanging on its end. In the last line, the relation of *Rad* to the solution has caused problems; some critics think that the scribe made an error and that the word should read *Rod*, an upright pole, but *Rad* (riding, journey) seems to me quite appropriate. The identity of the other two 'fitting runes' can only be guessed at – a game for academics.

Riddle 59

This is the second and more long-winded of the two riddles concerning church plate (the other is Riddle 48) and most critics accept the solution *chalice*. The turning of the ring (line 5) has not been explained satisfactorily; it probably refers to the holding of the chalice (and by inference the drinking of Christ's blood) and perhaps to the act of passing it to the next communicant.

Riddle 30b

See note to Riddle 30a. The textual differences between the two riddles are very small; the translation is identical.

Riddle 60

These lines precede the text of 'The Husband's Message', a poem in which a rune-stave speaks, asking a woman to sail south and join her exiled husband; some critics believe that they in fact constitute the first part of that poem, but I have followed the editors of *The Anglo-Saxon Poetic Records* in taking them to be a separate riddle. *Reed* seems the obvious answer – growing on a lonely shore, cut into a flute, and used as a pen. The riddle has similarities to Symphosius' Riddle 2: 'I am the riverbank's sweet mistress and the deep water's neighbour; I sing softly to the Muses. When I am bathed in black and grasped by a scholar's fingers, I am the tongue's messenger.'

Riddle 61

Helmet, or maybe *kirtle*, is the ostensible-answer and *vagina* is the innuendo-answer. The last half-line, 'Now guess what I mean', clearly signals the poet's intention to be ambiguous.

Riddle 62

This riddle has made commentators squirm. *Gimlet*, *burning arrow*, *poker* and *brand* have been suggested; but although this kind of sidetrack is clearly intended, the answer *penis* is unambiguous. Lines 5–6a refer to masturbation rather than an oiled tow wrapped round an arrow or a piece of cloth round a burning poker. The implication of 'southerner' in line 6 has not been established; some critics think the word *superne* means simply a foreign man, or a servant; someone, anyhow, whose behaviour is un-English!

Riddle 63

The text of the second half of this riddle is too defective to translate. The first half is intact and reads:

> I must often (and gracefully) gratify
> retainers in the hall when I'm taken round,
> gleaming with gold, where warriors carouse.
> Sometimes in the closet, when we're on our own,
> a loyal servant kisses my mouth;
> with his fingers he presses, embraces me,
> he works his will . . .

A *drinking-vessel* of some sort is clearly intended, and the riddle also contains sexual innuendo. Aldhelm's Riddle 80, *glass wine-cup*, has been cited as an analogue. Part of it reads: 'Many men want to clasp my neck with their right hands and to hold my slippery body in their fingers. But when I bring sweet kisses to their lips, laying them on the mouths which press close to me, I upset their minds and bring their staggering footsteps to a fall.'

Riddle 64

This riddle is six lines long and contains fifteen runes. It is clearly a companion to Riddle 19 in as much as the basic constituents are a man and his hawk. No translation is offered, for the meaning of some of the runes and the solution to the riddle are enigmatic in the extreme, and the riddle is also unsatisfying as a poem.

Riddle 65

Onion. This short riddle is as successful in its own way as its 'pair', Riddle 25. The original is attractively staccato:

Cwico waes ic, ne cwaeð ic wiht   cwele ic efne seþeah.
Ær ic waes, eft ic cwom.   Æghwa mec reafað,
hafað mec on headre,   ond min heafod scireþ . . .

Symphosius' Riddle 40 is a probable source: 'I bite those who bite me; otherwise I don't bite anyone. But many people are prepared to bite me who bite them. No one is afraid of my bite, since I don't have any teeth.'

Riddle 66

Creation. These lines incorporate some of the ideas and images developed in Riddle 40.

Riddle 67

I've heard of an object appertaining to God,
a marvellous creature, mysterious words . . .
(*lines 3–8 defective*)
          . . . I've become
a teacher of nations. For which reason now
. . . I may live life everlasting
in diverse, distant places, for as long as men
roam about earth's quarters. I've seen it
often, adorned with gold, treasure, silver,
where men sat drinking. Let him who can –
the most discerning – say what this object is.

The middle part of the riddle is too defective to be translated. The surviving lines suggest the solution *Bible*.

Riddle 68

All but two critics take Riddles 68 and 69 to be one riddle, with an answer involving the idea of running water becoming ice. But in *The Anglo-Saxon Poetic Records*, Krapp and Dobbie point out that 'they are written as separate riddles in the MS, and there is nothing in the texts of the two riddles which would justify us in associating them.' The two lines of this riddle are:

> I watched a creature going on its way;
> its clothes were as fine as they were curious.

They closely resemble the opening lines of Riddle 36 and are perhaps the start of a riddle the remainder of which was overlooked by the scribe, or already lost.

Riddle 69

Probably *ice*. See note to Riddle 68.

Riddle 70

Shepherd's pipe or *harp*. If line 2a refers to the holes for fingering, the answer is likely to be a shepherd's pipe; but lines 2b–4a favour harp.

Riddle 71

> A man of influence owns me, red gold
> clothes me, I'm a tough, sheer place.
> My station was once amongst shining
> flowers; now I'm the leavings
> of fire and file, firmly fastened,
> embellished with wire thread. He who thrusts
> against the gold will sometimes grieve
> at my onslaught when I, adorned with rings,
> smash [an heirloom] ...

The text of the last two and a half lines of this riddle is too damaged to be translated. A. J. Wyatt's description of this riddle as '*iron, first in the ore, then made into a weapon*', is unlikely to be bettered. There has been much inconclusive discussion as to whether the 'tough, sheer place' in line 2 refers to the blade itself or to the precipitous site from which the ore was quarried.

Riddle 72

The text of lines 1–5a of this riddle is defective. *Ox* is widely accepted as the solution, although an argument has been made out for *axle and wheels*.

Riddle 73

Lines 9–21 of this riddle are damaged and, although there is no break in the manuscript, the sense in line 24 suggests a word or two has been lost. The surviving lines read:

> In a field I quickened and increased, where soil
> and the clouds of heaven fed me, until,
> when I was old, fierce enemies
> changed me from what I'd been, alive;
> they altered my estate, moved me from the earth
> and, against my nature, made me
> bow at times to the will of butchers.
> Now in my master's hands I'm busy . . .
> [*lines 9–21 defective*]
> cherishes me and in the skirmish fights
> with skilful control. Everyone knows
> that I'm one of the daring, and deft
> as a thief, under the brain-house [. . .]
> Sometimes, in full sight, I streak
> towards a stronghold that has been swathed in peace.
> Fleet of foot, the warrior turns
> and hurries from that place – he's aware
> of my ways. Say what my name is.

Lance is accepted by all commentators except Moritz Trautmann, who prefers *battering-ram*. It is true that there are some similarities between this riddle and Riddle 53.

Riddle 74

Commentators have argued for *cuttlefish*, *water*, *siren* and *swan*. There is no way of clinching the case one way or other, but Frederick Tupper has certainly advanced an interesting case for *siren*:

> The Siren is both aged and young: centuries old and yet with the face of a girl. It is not only a woman but sometimes a man. At an early period of the Middle Ages the Teutonic conception of a fish-woman or mermaid met and mingled with the classical idea of a bird-maiden ... Every student of myths knows that when Ulysses or the Argonauts had passed in safety, the Sirens threw themselves into the sea, and were transformed into rocks.

Riddle 75

> I saw a quick one coursing down a track
> DNUH

Like Riddle 68, this may be the beginning of a longer riddle now lost; and like Riddle 19, the answer is achieved by reversing the order of the runes, which in the text read DNLH. Mackie would solve as HæLeND, 'Saviour'. Every other commentator emends the L to U and reads HUND, 'dog'.

Riddle 76

As with the previous riddle, these may simply be the first words of something longer. Mackie has suggested *hen* as the solution, and if one is to take the riddle as being complete (like Riddle 69), it cannot be bettered.

Riddle 77

Oyster. The text of the last half-line is damaged. The loquacious 'Fisherman' in Ælfric's *Colloquy* talks of catching 'eels and pike, minnows and turbot, trout and lampreys . . . herrings and salmon, porpoises and sturgeon, oysters and crabs, mussels, winkles, cockles, plaice and flounders and lobsters, and many similar things'.

Riddle 78

Only about twenty scattered words survive of this damaged eight-line riddle, and their translation serves no purpose. But parallels between Riddle 77 and what survives of this riddle suggest that the solution is *oyster*.

Riddle 79

This consists of one line:

> I'm a lord's possession and pleasure.

This is either a variation of the first line of Riddle 80 which begins with the same words (*Ic eom æpelinges*, 'I am of a lord') or another incomplete riddle.

Riddle 80

Horn is now widely agreed on, but *falcon*, *hawk*, *spear* and *sword* have also been suggested. See note to Riddle 14.

Riddle 81

Most commentators accept *weathercock*, which, with a bell (see note to Riddle 4) and a sundial, was one of the trappings of a well-equipped church. The stoic melancholy of this cameo is essentially Anglo-Saxon and echoes the tone of longer elegiac poems, such as 'The Wanderer':

Time and again at the day's dawning
I must mourn all my afflictions alone.
There is no one still living to whom I dare open
the doors of my heart. I have no doubt
that it is a noble habit for a man
to bind fast all his heart's feelings with silence,
whatever his impulse, his inclinations.

Riddle 82

Of the original six lines, four fragments remain. They read:

A creature is . . .
. . . quick, devours a great deal,

*

. . . skin nor flesh, on its feet goes

*

the meals of each man it must . . .

Clearly, no solution is possible; there is not really sufficient evidence to support Holthausen's suggestion, *crab*.

Riddle 83

Ore is widely accepted as the answer to this rather obscure riddle. The text of the first eight lines has been the subject of many emendations, and any translation of them will contain some degree of speculation (the postulated restorations are printed in square brackets). The 'keeper of fire' in lines 2 and 4–5 has been taken by some commentators to be Tubal-cain (Genesis 4: 22), but it could equally be a reference to Surt, who, in Norse mythology, ruled over Muspellheim (the world of fire). He already existed at the creation, when the worlds of fire and ice merged in the great chasm of Ginnungagap and life was first engendered.

Riddle 84

Water. Lines 11b–20 and 43–56 are badly damaged and cannot be translated; there is also a break in the sense in line 34, and a half-line is thought to be missing. The last surviving lines are fresh but overall the riddle is repetitive and rather wooden.

Riddle 85

Fish and river. Symphosius' Riddle 12, *Flumen et Piscis*, is the probable source of this riddle. It reads: 'On earth there is a home that echoes again and again with a clear sound. The home itself resounds, but the silent guest [*or* host] makes no noise. Yet the guest [*or* host] and the home both run on together.'

Riddle 86

Most critics accept *one-eyed seller of garlic*; it makes one recall the occasional Breton onion-seller now seen no longer on London streets, precarious on his bicycle, draped in his wares. Symphosius' Riddle 95 is taken to be a source: 'Now you can see what you can hardly believe; he has one eye but many thousands of heads. He sells what he has; where will he buy what he doesn't have?'

Riddle 87

I saw a strange creature; it had a huge stomach,
forcefully squeezed. A stalwart servant
with horny hands waited upon it; I thought him
a godlike warrior, at once he grasped
heaven's tooth . . .
he blew in its eye; it barked,
its will weakened. Nevertheless it would . . .

*

Bellows appears to be the most likely solution because of the marked similarities between this riddle and Riddle 37, and one can set aside the solutions *cask* and *cooper* with reasonable confidence. Line 5b is missing and line 8 damaged. 'Heaven's tooth' (assuming the text is accurate in the first instance) is a striking metaphor, but its precise meaning remains uncertain; a parallel has been drawn with *As You Like It*, II, vii, 177:

> Blow, blow, thou winter wind,
> Thou art not so unkind
>   As man's ingratitude;
> Thy tooth is not so keen,
> Because thou art not seen,
>   Although thy breath be rude.

Riddle 88

[*lines 1–8 defective*]
but there I towered, where my brother and I
had grown together; we two were sturdy.
Our station was the more select, the higher
because of the ornaments. Often the wood concealed us.
on dark nights the canopy of forest trees
shielded us from showers; God shaped us,
Now our kin will succeed us, mighty
as we are – younger brothers
will deprive us of our home. I am
unique on middle-earth; my back
is dark and strange. I stand on wood
at one end of the table. My brother isn't here
but, separated from him, I must stay
and stand alone at the table's end;
I don't know in which quarter or country
my brother lives as one of man's possessions,
he who once lived high beside me.
We always fought together.
We butted and rutted together; never

did either display his strength alone
or we would have both been defeated.
Now monsters eat at my insides,
    they gouge out my guts; I cannot escape,
He who searches will find riches in the spoor
            . . . soul's gain.

The answer is either *antler* or *inkhorn*, or both. The first
eight lines are too badly damaged to reconstitute and the last
line is also defective. The other (and superior) riddle relating
to an antler/inkhorn is Riddle 93.

Riddle 89

Less than twenty words survive of this ten-line riddle. No
translation is offered since they give no real idea as to the
solution and embody no memorable images.

Riddle 90

This riddle is in Latin. It translates literally:

It seemed to me a wonder, the wolf is held by the lamb; / the lamb
fell on to the rock and takes the bowels of the wolf. / Then might I
stand and sorrow, I have seen the great glory, / two wolves standing
and weeping for the third; / they have four feet, they see with seven
eyes.

The meaning of these five lines, written in six-stress lines
with some medial rhyme, has caused great perplexity, and no
commentator has come up with a solution that has found
favour with any other. Perhaps most interesting is Henry
Morley's apocalyptic explanation: 'The marvel of the Lamb
that overcame the wolf and tore its bowels out is of the Lamb
of God who overcame the devil and destroyed his power.' He
goes on to equate the 'four feet' to the four Gospels, the

'seven eyes' to the Book of Revelation and the 'two wolves' to the Old and New Testaments. Maybe, though, this is all too far-fetched. Bradley noted, 'I am strongly disposed to think it most probable that the reference is to circumstances well known to the author and to his readers, but to us quite unknown and unconjecturable'; and there, for the moment, the matter rests.

Riddle 91

Key, without the innuendo that characterizes Riddle 44. Symphosius' Riddle 4 is probably an analogue: 'I bring great power with my little strength. I open closed houses, but I close opened ones up again. I protect the home for the master, but I am protected by him in turn.'

Riddle 92

Almost five of the original seven lines survive. They read:

> I was the boast of brown ones; a tree in the forest,
> lofty life-bearer; earth's offspring;
> man's cause of joy and woman's message;
> treasure in your home. Now I'm the happy
> weapon of a warrior, with a ring . . .

The answer is widely taken to be a *beech*. The shape-changing form of this riddle, which seeks to confuse by being so many different things, is reminiscent of Riddles 30a and 40. Frederick Tupper argues that 'the boast of brown ones' may be the beech-mast on which swine subsist; line 3, rather reminiscent of the opening of 'The Husband's Message', might refer to a rune-stave, and 'treasure in your home' could be any prized domestic object made of wood. When the Germanic tribes first came to Britain, the land lay largely under great forests of ash, oak, and beech, such as the Weald which stretched from Hampshire to Kent and was 120 miles long and 30 miles wide, Selwood, Wychwood, Sherwood and the Chilterns.

Riddle 93

Ink container made from a stag's horn is accepted by all commentators except those who prefer a less specific answer, such as *horn* or *antler*. The text of lines 1–8 and lines 32b–35 is defective; I have indicated the rather uneasy change from third to first person singular in line 14 by dividing that line; lines 23–4 ('I suffer pain from all those / that have bitten the shield') appears to mean that the iron weapons that have, or might have, bitten into battle-shields now hollow out the horn; the 'preying enemy' in the following line is clearly a quill that as a feather supported the raven or the eagle, which, with the wolf, were the conventional (and doubtless actual) beasts of battle. Despite the textual difficulties and Paull F. Baum's fair comment that 'the lines are ambitiously elaborate and leave the impression that the writer's reach exceeded his grasp,' the riddle contains some extremely fresh images and is altogether more noble than its counterpart, Riddle 88.

Riddle 94

Several critics, including the editors of *The Anglo-Saxon Poetic Records*, believe that, as with Riddles 40 and 66, the answer to this riddle is *Creation*. The text of the six lines is badly damaged but, because it contains attractive images and is strangely satisfying in its fragmentary form, a translation is offered. Postulated restorations are included in square brackets:

> [I am the] shaper . . .
> higher than heaven . . .

> ... more brilliant than the sun,
> ... [stronger than] steel,

sharper than salt ...
loved more than all this light, brighter than [a fleece.]

Riddle 95

Riddle, *moon* and *wandering singer* have been proposed. It would be pleasant to think the poet or poets who composed the *Exeter Book* riddle collection rounded it off with a riddle about a riddle, but neither this nor the other proposals are very convincing. The poem ends:

> ic swaþe hwilum
> mine bemiþe   monna gehwylcum

'I sometimes conceal my tracks from all humankind.' Because the text is evidently corrupt, those tracks are rather more blurred than the poet intended. What *wiht* or creature, animate or inanimate, can have made them? Who can say?

MORE ABOUT PENGUINS
AND PELICANS

Penguinews, which appears every month, contains details of all the new books issued by Penguins as they are published. From time to time it is supplemented by our stocklist, which includes around 5,000 titles.

A specimen copy of *Penguinews* will be sent to you free on request. Please write to Dept EP, Penguin Books Ltd, Harmondsworth, Middlesex, for your copy

In the U.S.A.: For a complete list of books available from Penguins in the United States write to Dept CS, Penguin Books, 625 Madison Avenue, New York, New York 10022.

In Canada: For a complete list of books available from Penguins in Canada write to Penguin Books Canada Ltd, 2801 John Street, Markham, Ontario L3R 1B4.

In Australia: For a complete list of books available from Penguins in Australia write to the Marketing Department, Penguin Books Australia Ltd, P.O. Box 257, Ringwood, Victoria 3134.

SOME EARLY MEDIEVAL WORKS IN
PENGUIN CLASSICS

THE PENGUIN CLASSICS

Each year we are glad to add a few more titles to our ever-expanding list of Classics. This does not just mean works by Latin and Greek writers, but the most comprehensive collection ever of classic works from all countries – China, Japan, India and Iceland as well as Europe – all in new translations.

Here are some of the titles we are publishing in the next few months.

Schiller
THE ROBBERS AND WALLENSTEIN
Translated by F. J. Lamport

Rousseau
REVERIES OF THE SOLITARY WALKER
Translated by Peter France

Marivaux
UP FROM THE COUNTRY/INFIDELITIES
THE GAME OF LOVE AND CHANCE
Translated by Leonard Tancock and David Cohen

Anatole France
THE GODS WILL HAVE BLOOD
Translated by Frederick Davies

Turgenev
SPRING TORRENTS
Translated by Leonard Schapiro

THREE SANSKRIT PLAYS
Translated by Michael Coulson

Shikibu
THE TALE OF GENJI Volumes I and II
Translated by Edward Seidensticker